MURDER . . .
AMERICAN-STYLE!

Maigret hadn't the least idea of the identity of the man who had been tossed out onto the sidewalk of Rue Fléchier. He didn't even know if the man was dead or not. As for the second car, the one which had picked up the corpse or the wounded man, it was still more anonymous. Who were the occupants of that car? Why had they taken the risk of making off with the body? If the man was dead, what had they done with the corpse? If not, where was he being cared for? It was one of the rare investigations in which, at the outset, there was no clue. These people had apparently crossed the Atlantic to settle some scores about which the French police knew nothing.

MAIGRET
AND THE GANGSTERS

GEORGES SIMENON

Translated from the French
by Louise Varèse

AVON BOOKS  NEW YORK

AVON BOOKS
A division of
The Hearst Corporation
105 Madison Avenue
New York, New York 10016

First Avon Books Printing: October 1988

MAIGRET
AND THE GANGSTERS

One

"All right . . . all right . . . Yes, of course . . . Certainly . . . I'll do my best. . . . That's right. . . . Well then, good-by . . . What? I said good-by. . . . Quite all right . . . Good-by . . ."

For the tenth time at least—he hadn't kept count—Maigret hung up the receiver, relighted his pipe, gave a reproachful glance at the prolonged cold rain outside his window, and, picking up his pen, bent over the report begun more than an hour ago and still with less than half a page written.

Actually, as he began writing, he was thinking of something else; he was thinking of the rain, of that particular kind of rain that is the forerunner of the real winter cold and that has a way of creeping down your neck, into your shoes, of falling in great drops off the brim of your hat, a cold-in-the-head rain, dirty and dreary, that makes people want to stay at home, where you see them looking like ghosts behind their windows.

Is it boredom that impels them to telephone at such times? Of the eight or ten calls, almost in succession, there hadn't been three that were of the least use. And the bell was ringing again. Maigret looked at the instrument as if tempted to demolish it with his fist, finally barking:

"Hello?"

"Madame Lognon insists on speaking to you personally."

"Madame who?"

1

"Lognon."

On such a foul day and with his nerves already on edge, it seemed like some kind of practical joke, suddenly hearing on the wire the name of the man they had nicknamed Old Grouch, the most dismal man in the Paris police, so proverbially unlucky that some of the men insisted he had the evil eye.

And it wasn't even Lognon on the phone, but Madame Lognon. Maigret had met her only once, at their apartment on Place Constantin-Pecqueur in Montmartre. Since then, he no longer resented the man, although he still avoided him as much as possible, but pitied him from the bottom of his heart.

"Put her on . . . Hello! Madame Lognon?"

"Excuse me for disturbing you, Superintendent . . ."

She pronounced each syllable with affected care, like people do who want to prove they have had a good education. Maigret noticed that the date was Thursday, the sixteenth of November. The black marble clock on the mantelpiece pointed to eleven o'clock in the morning.

"I should never have taken the liberty of insisting upon speaking to you personally if I had not had an imperative reason. . . ."

"Yes, of course."

"You know us, Superintendent, my husband and myself. You know that . . ."

"Yes, madam."

"I simply must see you, Superintendent. Terrible things are happening, and I am frightened. If it weren't for my health, I would rush right over to the Quai des Orfèvres. But, as you know, for years now I've been confined to this fifth floor of mine."

"Am I to understand that you would like me to come there?"

"Please do, Monsieur Maigret."

It was atrocious. She had said it politely but firmly.

"Your husband isn't at home?"

"He has disappeared."

"What! Lognon has disappeared? Since when?"

"I don't know. He is not at his office, and no one knows where he is. The gangsters were here again this morning."

"The what?"

"The gangsters. I will tell you all about it, even if it makes Lognon furious. I am too frightened."

"You mean to say that some men entered your apartment?"

"Yes."

"Broke in?"

"Yes."

"Did they take anything?"

"Some papers perhaps. I haven't looked."

"Did it happen this morning?"

"Half an hour ago. But the other two had already been here, the day before yesterday."

"What was your husband's reaction?"

"I haven't seen him since."

"I'll be right there."

Maigret still didn't believe it. Not really. He scratched his head, chose two pipes, which he slipped into his pocket, and opened the door to the inspectors' room.

"Anyone heard anything of Lognon lately?"

The name invariably raised a smile. No. No one had heard anything. Inspector Lognon, despite his fervent desire, did not belong to the Crime Squad on Quai des Orfèvres, but to the second district of the Ninth Arrondissement, and his office was at the police station on Rue la Rochefoucauld.

"If anyone asks for me, I'll be back in an hour. Is there a car outside?"

He slipped into his thick overcoat, found a small police car in the courtyard, gave the address on Place Constantin-Pecqueur. It was about as cheerful on the streets as under the glass dome of the Gare du Nord, and people walked along stoically, their legs drenched by the jets of water the cars kept swishing over the sidewalks.

It was an ordinary-looking apartment house, about a century old, with no elevator. Sighing, Maigret climbed the five flights; a door opened before he had time to knock; Madame Lognon, with red eyes and nose, ushered him into the apartment, murmuring:

"I am so grateful to you for coming! If you only knew how my poor husband admires you!"

It wasn't true. Lognon detested him. Lognon detested everyone who was lucky enough to work at the Quai des Orfèvres, all the inspectors, everyone who was a grade above him. He detested everyone older than he because they were older, and the young ones because they were younger. He . . .

"Sit down, Superintendent . . ."

She was short and thin, with untidy hair, and she was wearing a flannel dressing gown of a hideous shade of mauve. She had deep circles under her eyes, pinched nostrils, and she kept pressing her hand to her left side, like someone suffering from heart trouble.

"I thought it preferable not to touch anything, so that you could see for yourself. . . ."

The apartment was tiny: a dining room, living room, bedroom, kitchen, and bathroom, everything on a diminutive scale, with doors that couldn't quite open fully because of the furniture. A black cat was curled on the bed.

Madame Lognon had taken Maigret into the dining room, and it was obvious that the living room was never used. There was no silver in the open drawers of the sideboard, only papers, notebooks, and photographs, which had been left in wild disorder; letters were scattered over the floor.

"I think," he said, hesitating to light his pipe, "you'd better begin at the beginning. On the phone you spoke of gangsters."

Before answering, she said in a tone of long-suffering resignation:

"You may smoke your pipe if you like."

"Thank you."

"Well, you see, it was Tuesday morning . . ."

"In other words, day before yesterday?"

"Yes. Lognon is on night duty this week. Tuesday morning he came home about six o'clock, as usual. But, instead of going to bed as soon as he had eaten, he kept pacing up and down until it made me fairly dizzy."

"Did he seem worried?"

"You know how terribly conscientious he is, Superintendent. I keep telling him that he is much too conscientious, that he will ruin his health, and that no one will thank him for it. You must excuse me for speaking so frankly, but you will have to admit that he has never been treated as he deserves. He's a man who thinks of nothing but his duty, and frets himself to death. . . ."

"So on Tuesday morning . . ."

"At eight o'clock he went out to do the marketing. I am ashamed to be nothing but a helpless invalid, almost good for nothing, but it isn't my fault. The doctor forbids me to climb the stairs, and so of course Lognon has to buy what we need. It's no work for a man like him, I know. Every time, I . . ."

"Tuesday morning?"

"He did the shopping. Then he told me that he had to go back to his office, that he probably wouldn't be long and would sleep in the afternoon."

"He didn't say anything about this case he's working on?"

"He never talks about his work. If I'm unfortunate enough to ask him a question, he always says it's a professional secret."

"He hasn't been home since?"

"About eleven o'clock, yes."

"The same day?"

"Yes. Tuesday about eleven o'clock in the morning."

"Was he still nervous?"

"I don't know if he was nervous or if it was his cold, since he'd caught a head cold. I insisted he take care of it. He replied that he would later, when he had time, that he had to go out again, but would be home before dinner."

"Did he come home?"

"Oh, but wait! My God! I've just thought! What if I never see him again! And to think of the way I reproached him. I said he never worried about his wife only about his work. . . ."

Resigned, Maigret waited, uncomfortable on a flimsy straight-backed chair, not daring to tilt back for fear of breaking it.

"It was perhaps half an hour after he left—not even that, toward one o'clock—that I heard footsteps on the stairs. I thought it was the woman on the sixth floor, a person who, between ourselves . . ."

"Yes. Footsteps on the stairs . . ."

"They stopped on my landing. I had just gone back to bed, as the doctor ordered me to do after meals. Someone knocked at the door, and I didn't answer. Lognon has warned me never to answer unless people tell their names. No one can work the way my husband does without making enemies, can they? I was surprised when I heard the door open, then steps in the hall, then in the dining room. There were two of them, two men looking into my bedroom, staring at me still there in bed."

"Did you get a good look at them?"

"I ordered them to leave, threatened them with the police; I even reached for the telephone, which was on the table by my bed."

"And then?"

"One of them, the little one, pointed a revolver at me and said something in a language I didn't understand, probably English."

"What did they look like?"

"I don't know how to describe them. They were very well dressed. They were both smoking cigarettes. They kept their hats on. They seemed surprised not to find something or somebody.

" 'If it's my husband you're looking for . . .' I began. But they didn't listen. The tall one went all over the apartment while the other stayed watching me. I remember they looked under the bed and in the closets."

"Didn't they go through the drawers?"

"Not those two, no. They didn't stay more than five minutes, didn't ask any questions, and calmly left as if their visit had been perfectly natural. Of course I rushed over to the window, and I saw them arguing down on the sidewalk near a big black automobile. The tall one got in, and the other walked to the corner of Rue Caulaincourt. I think he went into the bar. I phoned my husband's office right away."

"Was he there?"

"Yes. He had just come in. I told him what had happened."

"Did he seem surprised?"

"It's hard to say. He's always queer on the telephone."

"Did he ask you to describe the two men?"

"Yes, and I did."

"Will you describe them again."

"They were both very dark, like Italians, but I'm sure it wasn't Italian they were speaking. I think the tall one was the boss, a handsome man, I must say, a little bit too stout, about forty. He looked as if he'd just come from the barber's."

"And the short one?"

"More vulgar. He had a broken nose, ears like a boxer's, and a gold front tooth. He wore a pearl-gray hat and a gray overcoat; the other one had a brand-new camel's-hair coat."

"Didn't your husband hurry right home?"

"No."

"Didn't he have the district police come over?"

"No, he didn't. He told me not to worry, even if he didn't come home for several days. I asked him what I'd do about food, and he said he'd attend to it."

"And did he?"

"Yes. The next morning, delivery boys brought everything I needed. They came back again this morning."

"You didn't hear from Lognon all day yesterday?"

"He telephoned me twice."

"And today?"

"Once, about nine o'clock."

"You don't know where he was when he phoned?"

"No. He never tells me where he is. I don't know how other inspectors are with their wives, but he . . ."

"Let's get to the visit you had this morning."

"Again I heard someone on the stairs."

"What time was it?"

"A little after ten. I didn't look at the clock. Perhaps ten-thirty."

"They were the same men?"

"There was only one. I'd never seen him before. He didn't knock, came right in as if he had the key. Maybe he had a passkey. I was in the kitchen preparing my vegetables. I got up and I saw him standing in the doorway.

" 'Don't move,' he said. 'And don't scream. I'm not going to hurt you.' "

"Did he have a foreign accent?"

"Yes. He made several mistakes in French. This one, I'm sure, was really an American, a tall, reddish-blond man with broad shoulders, and he was chewing gum. He looked all around with curiosity, as if he'd never been in a Paris apartment before. When he glanced in the living room he noticed right away the certificate Lognon received after twenty-five years in the police."

The certificate was in a black wooden frame ornamented in gold, with Lognon's name and title written in large round letters.

" 'So he's a cop,' the man said. 'Where is he?' I told him I didn't know, and he didn't seem to care. Then he began opening drawers and rummaging through papers, tossing them around so carelessly some fell on the floor.

"He found a photograph of my husband and me taken fifteen years ago. He looked at me and shook his head. Then he slipped the picture in his pocket."

"In short, he hadn't expected to find that your husband was a policeman?"

"He didn't seem exactly surprised, but I feel sure he didn't know it when he came."

"Did he ask what department he belonged to?"

"He asked me where he could find him. I said I didn't have the least idea, that my husband never talked to me about his work."

"He didn't insist?"

"He went on reading everything he could lay his hands on."

"Were your husband's credentials in a drawer?"

"Yes. The man put some of them in his pocket with the photograph. In the sideboard he found a bottle of Calvados and poured himself a big drink."

"That's all?"

"He looked under the bed, like the others, and in the closets. He went back to the dining room for another drink. Then he left, making me a most sarcastic bow."

"Did you notice if he was wearing gloves?"

"Pigskin glove, yes."

"And the other two?"

"I think they were wearing gloves too. The one who threatened me with his revolver was, I know."

"Did you look out the window again?"

"Yes. I saw him leave the house and join one of the others, the short one, who was waiting at the corner of Rue Caulaincourt. Right away I phoned the Rochefoucauld police station and asked to speak to Lognon. They told me they hadn't seem him this morning, that they didn't expect him, and when I insisted, they said he hadn't been there last night at all, though he's on night duty."

"Did you tell them what had happened?"

"No. Right away I thought of you, Superintendent. You see, I know Lognon better than anyone. He's a man who tries too hard. Till now he's never had the recognition he deserves, but he has often spoken of you. I know that you are not like the others, that you are not jealous of him, that . . . I'm frightened, Monsieur Maigret. He must have taken on someone stronger than himself, and, by this time, God knows where . . ."

The telephone rang in the bedroom. Madame Lognon gave a start.

"Will you excuse me, please?"

Maigret could hear her in a suddenly changed tone saying stiffly:

"Oh, it's you, is it? Where have you been? I telephoned your office, and they said you hadn't set foot in the place since yesterday. Superintendent Maigret is here. . . ."

Maigret, who had followed her, reached for the telephone.

"May I? . . . Hello! Lognon?"

The man on the other end of the wire remained silent, eyes stubborn, no doubt, lips set.

"Tell me, Lognon, where are you now?"

"At my office."

"I'm here in your apartment with your wife. I must have a talk with you. I'll stop off at Rochefoucauld on my way back. Wait there for me . . . What?"

He heard the Inspector stammering:

"Not here, Superintendent. I'll explain. . . ."

"Then be at the Quai des Orfèvres in half an hour."

He hung up, went to get his pipe, his hat.

"You don't think anything's wrong?"

And, as he looked at her without understanding, she added:

"He's so reckless, always trying to outdo himself, that sometimes . . ."

"Tell him to come in."

Lognon was drenched and covered with mud, as if he'd been wandering the streets all night, and he had such a cold that he had to keep his handkerchief in his hand all the time. He hung his head, like someone who expects to be raked over the coals, and remained standing in the middle of the room.

"Sit down, Lognon. I've just come from your place."

"What did my wife tell you?"

"Everything she knew, I suppose."

Lognon took advantage of the rather prolonged silence that followed to blow his nose, without daring to look at Maigret, and the Superintendent, aware of his touchiness, felt at a loss as to how to tackle him.

What Madame Lognon had said about her husband was not so far from the truth. The poor fool, by forever trying to do more, was always getting himself into hot water, and was convinced that the whole world was against him, that he was the victim of a concerted plot to keep him from being promoted and from at last enjoying the place he deserved on the Crime Squad of the Quai des Orfèvres.

It was all the more distressing because he wasn't stupid; he was really conscientious and the most honest man in the world.

"Is she in bed?" he finally asked.

"She was up when I arrived."

"Is she mad at me?"

"Look at me, Lognon. Relax. I know only what your wife told me, but it's enough to take one look at you to know something's wrong. You're not accountable to me directly, so whatever you've done is none of my business. But now that your wife has consulted me, wouldn't it be better to bring me up to date? What do you think?"

"I suppose so, yes."

"In that case, I must ask you to tell me everything. You understand? Not just a part, not *almost* everything."

"I understand."

"Fine. Don't you want to smoke?"

"I don't smoke."

That was true. Maigret had forgotten. He didn't smoke because the smell of tobacco made Madame Lognon sick.

"What do you know about these gangsters?"

To that, Lognon replied with conviction:

"I believe they really are gangsters."

"Americans?"

"Yes."

"How did you happen to get mixed up with them?"

"I don't really know myself. The way things are now, I might as well tell you everything, even if I lose my job."

He kept his eyes fixed on the desk, and his bottom lip was trembling.

"It was bound to happen sooner or later."

"What?"

"You know very well. They keep me because they can't help themselves, because they can't find an excuse, but for years they've been waiting to get me. . . ."

"Who?"

"Everybody."

"Oh, come now, Lognon."

"Yes, Superintendent."

"Will you please stop imagining you're being persecuted!"

"Excuse me."

"Stop hunching your shoulders and avoiding my eyes. That's better! Now talk to me like a man."

Lognon wasn't crying, but his cold made his eyes water, and it was irritating to see him continually putting his handkerchief to his nose.

"I'm listening."

"It happened Monday night, or, rather, early Tuesday morning."

"When you were on duty?"

"Yes. It was about one o'clock in the morning. I was on a surveillance."

"Where?"

"Right by the church of Notre-Dame-de-Lorette, up against the fence at the corner of Rue Fléchier."

"That isn't in your district, is it?"

"Just at the boundary. Fléchier is in the third district, but I was watching a little bar at the corner of Rue des Martyrs, which is in my district. I'd had a tip that a fellow came there nights to sell cocaine. Rue Fléchier is dark and almost deserted at that time of night. I was standing flat against the iron fence around the church. While I was waiting, a car turned the corner of Rue de Châteaudun, slowed up, stopped for a second not ten yards from me. Nobody in the car had any idea I was there. The door opened, and a body was tossed out onto the sidewalk; then the car made off down Rue Saint-Lazare."

"Did you get the number?"

"Yes. First I ran over to have a look at the body. I'd almost swear the man was dead, but I'm not sure. In the dark I felt his chest, and when I took my hand away, it was sticky with blood, still warm."

Maigret frowned, and murmured:

"I didn't see anything like that in the report."

"I know."

"This took place on the sidewalk of Rue Fléchier, consequently in the third district."

"Yes."

"How does it happen . . ."

"I'll explain. I realize I was wrong. Perhaps you won't believe me."

"What happened to the body?"

"That's just it. I'm coming to that. There wasn't a policeman in sight. The little bar was open not a hundred yards away. I went in to telephone."

"To whom?"

"To the police station of the third district."

"And did you?"

"I stopped at the counter to get a token. I happened to glance outside and I saw another car leaving Rue Fléchier and disappearing down Rue Notre-Dame-de-Lorette. It had stopped near where I'd left the body. So I ran out to try to get the number, but by that time it was too far away."

"A taxi?"

"I don't think so. It all happened very fast. I had a hunch. I ran over toward the church. The corpse wasn't there near the fence any longer."

"You didn't turn in an alarm?"

"No."

"Didn't it occur to you that by broadcasting the number of the first car, the police would have a chance of catching it?"

"I thought of that. But it seemed to me that the people who'd done this job weren't so dumb as to go around in the same car very long."

"You didn't draw up a report?"

Maigret had, of course, understood. For years and years poor Lognon had been waiting for something big to break, something that would put him in the limelight at last. It really seemed as if fate was against him. Although there were more crimes in his district than in any other, every time one was committed there, either it happened when he was off duty or else for some reason the Crime Squad would take over.

"I know it was wrong. I realized it almost at once, but because I hadn't turned in the alarm, by that time it was too late."

"Have you found the car?"

"In the morning I went to the Prefecture to look up the license number. The car belongs to a garage at the Porte Maillot. So I went up there. It's a garage that rents cars you drive yourself, either by the day or by the month."

"Had the car come back?"

"No. It had been rented two days before for an unspec-
ified length of time. I saw the form with the name and
address of the client, a certain Bill Larner, an American,
living at the Hotel Wagram, Avenue de Wagram."

"Did you find Larner at his hotel?"

"He had left the hotel about four o'clock in the morning."

"You mean that he was in his room until four o'clock
in the morning?"

"Yes."

"So he wasn't in the car?"

"He couldn't have been. The night clerk saw him come
in about midnight. He got a telephone call at half past
three and went right out."

"With his luggage?"

"No. He told the night clerk that he was going to the
station to meet a friend and would be back for breakfast."

"And naturally he hasn't come back."

"No."

"And the car?"

"It was found this morning near the Gare du Nord."

Once more Lognon blew his nose and looked penitently
at Maigret.

"I can only repeat that I was wrong. This is Thursday,
and ever since Tuesday morning I've been trying to figure
it out. I haven't been back home."

"Why?"

"My wife must have told you that they came just a little
after I left Tuesday. That's a clue, isn't it?"

Maigret let him go on talking.

"The way I see it, they must have caught sight of me
there in the dark after they'd dumped the body out on the
sidewalk. They figured I'd got the license number. I'm
talking about the first car, naturally, because there were
two. So they got rid of it in a hurry. Then they phoned
Bill Larner to let him know he'd probably be traced through
the garage."

Maigret was absently doodling on his blotter while he listened.

"And then?"

"I don't know. I'm only guessing. They must have scoured the papers and not found any mention of the affair."

"Have you any idea how they got on to you?"

"I can think of only one explanation, and it proves they know all the answers, that they're professionals. They must have kept a watch on the garage, saw me go in to ask about the car, and followed me. I went home for breakfast, and when they saw me come out again, they went up to the apartment."

"Where they hoped to find the body?"

"You think so too?"

"I don't know. . . . Why haven't you gone home since?"

"Because I suppose they're watching the building."

"Scared, Lognon?"

Lognon's face grew as red as his bulbous nose.

"I knew that's what people would think. But it isn't true. I wanted to keep my freedom of action. I took a room in a little hotel on Place de Clichy and kept in touch with my wife by phone. Since then I've been working night and day. I've been to a hundred hotels, first in the neighborhood of Avenue de Wagram, then around the Opéra. My wife gave me a description of the two men who came to the apartment. I went to the Resident Aliens Bureau of the Prefecture. During all this time I've kept up with my routine work."

"In short, you hoped to carry on the investigation on your own."

"At the beginning, yes. I believed I was capable of doing it. Now they can do what they like with me."

Poor Lognon! There were moments when, in spite of his forty-seven years and his unprepossessing appearance, he looked like a sulky boy, a boy at the awkward age, glowering furtively at grownups.

"Your wife had another visitor this morning, and since she couldn't reach you, she telephoned me."

Discouraged, the Inspector looked at Maigret, as much as to say that, considering the way matters stood, it was all the same to him.

"It wasn't either of the men who came Tuesday, but a tall, reddish-blond man. . . ."

"Bill Larner," growled Lognon. "That's the way he was described to me."

"When he left, he joined one of the others outside. He took away at least one photograph of you and probably some papers."

"I suppose I'll be called before the disciplinary board."

"That's something we'll discuss afterward."

"After what?"

"After the investigation."

His face still gloomy, Lognon frowned incredulously.

"The first thing to do now is to find these gangsters."

"You mean me, too?"

Maigret didn't answer, and Lognon blew his nose for three whole minutes.

When he left the room, anyone would have sworn he'd been crying.

TWO

It was almost five o'clock before Maigret's call came through. The lights had been turned on long ago, and people traipsing in and out all day had left the floors wet and muddy. In such weather, does tobacco really taste so different, or was Maigret, too, coming down with a cold?

He heard the operator on the other end of the line say, in English, pronouncing his name as if it had at least three *t*'s at the end:

"Paris calling. Police Judiciaire. Superintendent Maigret on the line."

Then, almost instantly, J. J. MacDonald's youthful, cheerful, friendly tones:

"Hello there, Jules!"

This was something Maigret had more or less inured himself to during his visit to the United States, but it still gave him a queer feeling, and he had to take a long breath before replying in the same vein:

"Hello, Jimmy!"

MacDonald was one of J. Edgar Hoover's chief assistants in the FBI in Washington. He had been Maigret's guide through most of the principal U.S. cities. He was a tall fellow with bright blue eyes, whose necktie was usually in his pocket, his jacket on his arm.

Over there, after ten minutes, everybody called you by your Christian name.

"How's Paris?"

"It's raining."

"Here it's bright and sunny."

"Say, Jimmy, I need some information and I don't want to waste the taxpayers' money. First, have you ever heard of a certain Bill Larner?"

"You mean *Sweet* Bill?"

"I don't know. I know only the name Bill Larner. According to his description, he's about forty."

"That must be Sweet Bill. He left the country about two years ago, and he spent a couple of months in Havana before sailing for Europe."

"Dangerous?"

"Not a killer, if that's what you mean, but one of the best swindlers in America. No one can beat him at getting fifty grand out of a sucker by promising him a million. So you've got him in your country now?"

"He's in Paris."

"Perhaps, with your laws, you'll be able to get him. Here, we've never succeeded in getting enough evidence against him and we've always had to let him go. Do you want me to send you his records?"

"If possible. That's not all. I'll read you a list of names. Stop me if you know any of them."

Maigret had set Janvier to work. The Police Judiciaire had procured a list of all the passengers who had landed at Le Havre and Cherbourg in the past few weeks, and the passport inspectors had supplied information that made it possible to eliminate a certain number of names.

"Can you hear me?"

"As if you were in the next room."

At the tenth name, MacDonald stopped his French colleague.

"Did you say Cinaglia?"

"Charles Cinaglia."

"Is he there too?"

"He landed two weeks ago."

"You'd better keep your eye on that baby. He's been in prison five or six times, and if he'd got what he deserved, he'd have gone to the chair long ago. He's a killer. All we've been able to get him for is illegal possession of arms, assault and battery, vagrancy, et cetera.''

''What does he look like?''

''Short, husky, always well dressed, a diamond ring, high heels. Broken nose and cauliflower ears.''

''It seems he arrived at the same time as a certain Cicero, who had the cabin next to his.''

''Sure! Tony Cicero worked with Charlie in St. Louis. But Tony never does any of the dirty work. He's the brains.''

''Have you any data on them?''

''Enough to start a library. I'll send along the most interesting. Also photographs. They'll leave by plane tonight.''

The other names meant nothing to MacDonald, and after another exchange of ''Jules'' and ''Jimmy,'' Maigret's voice ceased to echo through an office in Washington, where the sun was shining and where it was not yet time for lunch.

Because he had to consult the Chief Commissioner of the Police Judiciaire about another case, Maigret picked up a handful of papers and left his office. Crossing the waiting room, he felt there was someone in one of the dim corners. He turned to look and was surprised to see Lognon sitting there. The Inspector gave him a wan smile.

It was almost six o'clock. The offices were beginning to empty, and the permanently dusty entrance hall was deserted.

Ordinarily, if Lognon wanted to speak to Maigret, he would telephone, or else, if he happened to be in the neighborhood, would send up his name or even go up to the Superintendent's office, for he was more or less one of them even though officially he did not belong to the Quai des Orfèvres.

But not today! He had made a mistake, and he felt the

need to appear abnormally humble and to sit there like a poor boob until someone happened to notice him.

Maigret almost lost his patience. He felt that this humility was just another form of arrogance. The man seemed to be saying:

"You see! I've been to blame. You could have had me up before the disciplinary board. You have been good to me. I appreciate it and I am putting myself in the place I deserve, that of a poor beggar who lives on charity."

It was idiotic! It was Lognon through and through, and it was perhaps this trait in him that made any attempt to help him so discouraging. Even his cold he endured as a kind of penance!

He had gone home to change. His suit was just as drab as the one he'd been wearing that morning, and his shoes were already soaking wet. As for his overcoat, it was probably the only one he had.

If he had been scouring the city, he had certainly taken buses, waiting for them on street corners in the pouring rain *on purpose*.

"Naturally, *I* don't have an automobile at my disposal! Naturally, I can't . . . I don't want to take taxis. It's beneath my dignity to argue with the cashier at the end of every month. He always acts as if I were cheating on my expense account. I don't cheat. I'm an honest man, a conscientious man."

Maigret rapped out:

"You want to talk to me?"

"There's no hurry. Whenever you have time."

"Then go and wait for me in my office."

"I'll wait here."

The idiot! The dreary idiot! Yet it was impossible not to feel sorry for him. He was certainly very unhappy. He was eating his heart out.

When Maigret got back from the Chief's office twenty minutes later, Lognon hadn't budged; he hadn't smoked;

he had just sat there in the waiting room dripping like an umbrella.

"Come in. Sit down."

"I thought perhaps I'd better tell you what I've found out. This noon you didn't give me any definite instructions, and I understood that I was to do the best I could."

Too much humility again. Usually, of course, it was too much pride that made him unbearable.

"I went back to the Hotel Wagram. Bill Larner still hadn't showed up, but I got some information on him."

Maigret almost said, "So did I."

But what was the use?

"He's been living in the same room for nearly two years. I had a look at it. His luggage is still there. Apparently he took only a briefcase containing his papers. I didn't find any letters or passport in the drawers. His clothes all have labels of the best tailors. He spent money freely, gave big tips, and he entertained a lot of women, all the same kind, the kind you see in night clubs. The concierge said he seemed to like brunettes, preferably small, but plump."

Lognon very nearly blushed.

"I asked if friends came to see him sometimes. He said no. On the other hand, he got a lot of telephone calls. No letters. None at all. One of the desk clerks thinks he often went to eat at Pozzo's on Rue des Acacias. He's seen him there several times."

"Did you go to Pozzo's?"

"Not yet. I thought maybe you'd rather go yourself. I questioned the clerks at the post office on Avenue Niel. That's where he received his mail poste restante. Mostly letters from the United States. He got letters there again yesterday morning. They hadn't seen him today, but there isn't any mail for him."

"That's all?"

"Almost. I went to the Resident Aliens Bureau and found his record, since he regularly received his alien resident's card. He was born in Omaha—I don't know where that is, but it's in America—and he's forty years old.''

Lognon took from his wallet one of those passport photographs that foreigners have to bring with them in triplicate when they apply for their card. According to the photo, Bill Larner was a good-looking man with lively, laughing eyes. He looked as if he enjoyed life, and was slightly overweight.

"That's all I could find out. I looked for fingerprints in my apartment but there weren't any. They used a passkey to get in.''

"Is your wife feeling better?''

"She had an attack after I got home. She's in bed.''

Why couldn't he say it in a natural tone of voice? He seemed to be apologizing for the state of his wife's health, as if he were responsible, as if the whole world held him personally to blame.

"I forgot. I stopped at the garage at the Porte Maillot to show them the photograph. It's Larner, all right, who rented the car. When he paid the deposit, he took out a wad of money, nothing smaller than thousand-franc notes, it seems. The car was standing right there, so I examined it. They'd washed it, but you could still see spots on the back seat that were probably blood.''

"No trace of a bullet?''

"I didn't find any.''

He blew his nose, the way some women who have had their share of troubles will suddenly shed a few tears in the middle of a conversation.

"What do you intend to do now?'' Maigret asked, careful not to look at him.

Just the sight of his red nose and watery eyes made his own eyelids prick, and he had the feeling that he was catching Lognon's cold. He couldn't help being sorry for him. The man had just spent several hours in the cold rain scouring Paris from one end to the other. A few telephone calls would have achieved the same results, but what was the use of telling him so? Didn't he have to punish himself?

"I'll do whatever you tell me to do. I'm grateful to you for still allowing me to help in the investigation. I know I've no right to."

"Is your wife waiting for you for dinner?"

"She never waits for me. And even if she were waiting . . ."

Maigret felt like shouting, "For God's sake, stop it!"

But instead, in spite of himself, he proposed what amounted to a gift.

"Listen, Lognon. It's about half past six. I'll phone my wife that I won't be home, and we'll go and have dinner together at Pozzo's. Maybe we'll dig up something there."

He went into the next room to leave instructions with Janvier, who was on duty, shrugged into his heavy overcoat, and a few minutes later they were waiting for a taxi on a corner of the quay. It was still raining. Paris gave one the impression of being in a tunnel in the train: the lights seemed unnatural; people hugged the walls as if they were fleeing from some mysterious danger.

On the way, Maigret had an idea and stopped the taxi outside a bistro.

"I have to make a phone call. It will give us time for a quick drink."

"Do you need me inside?"

"No. Why?"

"I'd rather wait for you here. Drinking gives me heartburn."

It was a little bar for drivers, very warm and very smoky, with the telephone next to the kitchen.

"Is this the Resident Aliens Bureau? Is that you, Robin? Hello, old man. Will you look and see if the two names I'm going to give you are registered?"

He gave Cinaglia's and Cicero's names.

"All I need to know is if they've taken out residents' cards."

They hadn't. They hadn't been near the Prefecture, which seemed to indicate they didn't intend to stay long in Paris.

"Rue des Acacias."

He felt that this was his day for good deeds. In the taxi, he gave Lognon a full account of his activities.

"The two men who went to your place Tuesday, the dark ones, seem to be Charlie Cinaglia and Tony Cicero. They're evidently tied up with Larner. He got them the car, and it was Larner who went to your apartment the second time. Probably because the others didn't know any French."

"I thought of that too."

"The first time, they weren't looking for papers, but for a man, either dead or alive, the one they'd tossed out on the sidewalk of Rue Fléchier. That's why they looked under the bed and in the closets. When they didn't find anything, they wanted to know who you were, and where to find you, so they sent Larner, and he searched your drawers."

"Now they know that I belong to the police."

"That must have given them a jolt. And the newspapers' silence must have them worried too."

"Aren't you afraid they may leave Paris?"

"To be safe, I've alerted all the railway stations and airports and the highway police. Their description has been sent out, or, to be exact, Janvier is taking care of it at this moment."

Even in the darkness of the taxi, Maigret sensed Lognon's little smile.

And that's why he's called the great Maigret! he could be thinking. While a poor inspector like me tramps the streets when he's carrying out an investigation, all the famous inspector has to do is telephone Washington, order a lot of people around, notify railway stations and local police!

Poor old Lognon! Maigret felt like giving him a friendly

slap on the knee and saying, "Come on, Lognon, be yourself!"

As a matter of fact, he might be unhappy if he no longer
deserved the nickname Old Grouch. He needed to grouse
all the time, needed to convince himself that he was the
unluckiest man in the whole world.

The taxi came to a stop in the narrow Rue des Acacias,
in front of a restaurant with red-and-white-checked curtains at the door and windows. The minute he stepped
inside, Maigret seemed to get a whiff of the New York
Jimmy MacDonald had shown him. Pozzo's was not like
a Paris restaurant. It reminded him of the ones you find
on many of the streets around Broadway. It was so dimly
lit that it took some time before one could distinguish anything, and it left faces floating in a kind of chiaroscuro.

There was a row of high stools along the mahogany bar,
and small American and French flags were arranged between the bottles on the shelves. A radio was playing
softly. There were nine or ten tables, covered with red-
and-white-checked cloths like the curtains, and on the
paneled walls hung photographs of boxers and actors, especially boxers, most of them signed.

The place was almost empty at that hour. Two men at
the bar were playing with dice with the bartender. In the
rear, a couple sat eating spaghetti under the indifferent
eyes of the waiter, who was standing near the service window to the kitchen.

No one rushed forward to meet them. For an instant,
eyes turned toward the strange pair presented by Maigret
and the lean, lugubrious Lognon, and there was a special
silence, as though someone had given the warning when
they opened the door: "Watch it! Cops!"

Maigret hesitated about whether to sit at the bar, but,
after getting rid of his coat and hat, decided to take the
nearest table. There was an agreeable smell of highly sea-
soned cooking with a decided reek of garlic. The dice

were rolling again, but the bartender kept looking at the newcomers with a rather amused expression on his face.

Without a word, the waiter held out the menu.

"Do you like spaghetti, Lognon?"

"I'll take whatever you take."

"Give us two spaghettis to begin with."

"What kind of wine?"

"A bottle of Chianti."

His glance wandered over the photographs, and after a while he rose and went over to examine one of them more closely. It must have been taken many years ago. It showed a husky young boxer and was inscribed to Pozzo and signed "Charlie Cinaglia."

The man at the bar hadn't taken his eyes off Maigret. Without stopping his game, he called out:

"So you're interested in boxing?"

And Maigret came back with:

"In certain boxers, perhaps. You're Pozzo, aren't you?"

"And you're Maigret, I suppose."

All this very calmly and casually, like tennis players batting balls to each other before a match.

When the waiter came with the bottle of Chianti, Pozzo made another remark:

"I thought you never drank anything but beer."

He was short, almost bald, with a few hairs carefully brushed across the top of his head, and he had large prominent eyes, a nose as bulbous as Lognon's, and a clown's flexible mouth. With the two men facing him at the bar, he spoke Italian. They were both dressed in expensive bad taste, and Maigret would probably have found their names in his files. The younger was plainly a drug addict.

"Help yourself, Lognon."

"After you, Superintendent."

Had Lognon really never eaten spaghetti before? Was he doing it on purpose? He conscientiously imitated all Maigret's gestures, with the air of a guest who is determined to please his host.

"Do you like it?"

"It's not bad at all."

"Would you rather have something else?"

"No indeed. It must be very nourishing."

The spaghetti kept sliding off his fork, and the woman eating at the back of the restaurant couldn't help bursting out laughing. At the bar, the game had come to an end. The two customers shook hands with Pozzo, glanced at Maigret, and then strolled toward the door slowly, as if to prove they had nothing to fear, nothing on their conscience.

"Pozzo!"

"Yes, Superintendent."

The Italian was even shorter than he looked behind his bar. His legs were disproportionately short, and it was all the more noticeable because his trousers were too large.

He came up to the policeman's table wearing his genial business smile, a white napkin over his arm.

"So you like Italian cooking?"

Instead of replying, Maigret glanced over at the photograph of the boxer.

"Have you seen Charlie lately?"

"You know Charlie? Then you've been to America?"

"And you?"

"Me? I lived there for twenty years."

"In St. Louis?"

"In Chicago, in St. Louis, in Brooklyn."

"When did Charlie come here with Bill Larner?"

More and more Maigret was reminded of his stay in the United States, and he felt that Lognon was listening in some amazement to this conversation.

It was certainly not the way things would normally happen in France. Pozzo's attitude was not that of a proprietor of a more or less shady place being questioned by the police.

He stood there in front of them without ceremony, per-

fectly at ease, an ironic look in his bulging eyes. He made
a little face and scratched his head.

"So you know Bill too? Sweet Bill, eh? A nice guy."

"One of your good customers, isn't he?"

"You think so?"

He seated himself at their table.

"A glass, Angelino."

He poured himself some Chianti.

"Don't worry. The wine is on me. The dinner too. It
isn't every day I have the honor of entertaining Superintendent Maigret."

"You're enjoying yourself, Pozzo?"

"I always enjoy myself. I'm not like your friend here.
Has he just lost his wife?"

He contemplated Lognon with a look of false commis-
eration.

"Angelino! Bring these gentlemen *scaloppine alla fiorentina.* Tell Giovanni to do them the same as for me. You
like *scaloppine alla fiorentina,* Superintendent?"

"I met Charlie Cinaglia three days ago."

"Then you've just come from New York by plane?"

"Charlie was in Paris."

"Really? That shows you what people are. Ten years
ago I was his dear old Pozzo here, his dear old Pozzo
there. I think he even called me Papa Pozzo. Now he's in
Paris and doesn't even come to see me!"

"And Bill Larner? He hasn't come either? Or Tony Cicero?"

"What was that last name?"

He didn't even try to hide that he was kidding. Quite
the contrary. He was exaggerating on purpose, more and
more like a clown going through his routine. But when
you looked at him closely, you noticed that, in spite of all
his joking and his grimacing, his eyes remained hard and
watchful.

"It's funny. I've known lots of Tonys, but I don't recall
any Cicero."

"From St. Louis."

"You were in St. Louis? That's where I became an American citizen. I still am."

"But at this moment you are living in France. And the French government could very well take away your license."

"Why? Doesn't my place conform to all your health regulations? You can ask the local police. Never any trouble. No girls soliciting, either. In fact, the district inspector sometimes does me the honor of dining here with his missis. There aren't many people at this hour. It's too early. My clientele comes later. Now just tell me what you think of that *scaloppine.*"

"Do you have a telephone?"

"Naturally. It's in the back, at the left, the door next to the lavatory."

Maigret rose, went to the phone booth, and closed the door. He dialed the number of the Police Judiciaire and spoke in a low voice:

"Janvier? I'm at Pozzo's, the restaurant on Rue des Acacias. Will you tell the switchboard to keep someone on this line all evening? You have plenty of time. It won't be for another half hour. I want all the conversations taken down, especially if these three names are mentioned."

He dictated the names Cinaglia, Cicero, and Bill Larner.

"Nothing new?"

"Nothing. I'm having all the boardinghouse records searched."

When he got back to his table, he found Pozzo trying in vain to get a smile out of Lognon.

"So, you didn't come to see me just for my cooking, Superintendent?"

"Listen, Pozzo. Charlie and Cicero have been in Paris for two weeks, and you know it as well as I do. They probably met Larner here."

"I don't know Cicero, but if Charlie came here, he sure must have changed. I didn't recognize him."

"All right. For certain reasons, I want to have a little private talk with these gentlemen."

"All three?"

"This is serious. It's murder."

Pozzo crossed himself comically.

"You understand? We're not in America, where proof is hard to get."

"You hurt me, Superintendent. I never expected this from you. I really didn't."

And, holding up his glass:

"Your health! And to think I was so happy to meet you! I'd heard a lot about you, like everybody. I always said, 'There's a man who understands life.' Then you come to see me and you treat me as if you didn't know that Pozzo never hurt anybody. You talk to me about some boxer I haven't seen for ten or fifteen years, and you insinuate I don't know what!"

"That'll do! I'm not arguing today. I'm warning you. I said, 'Murder.' "

"Funny, I didn't see anything in the papers. Who was murdered?"

"It doesn't matter. If Charlie and Cicero have been here, if you have the least idea where they are now, I can have you up for aiding and abetting."

Pozzo shook his head sadly.

"To do that to me!"

"Have they been here?"

"When did you say they'd come to my place?"

"Have they been here?"

"So many people come here. At certain hours, all the tables are taken, and people wait outside on the street. I can't see everybody."

"Have they been here?"

"Listen. We'll make a deal, and you'll see Pozzo's a real friend. I promise if they set foot in here, I'll phone you immediately. Is that honorable? Tell me what this guy Cicero looks like.''

"Not necessary.''

"Then how am I supposed to recognize him? Can I ask all my customers for their passports? Can I do that? I'm married, I have a family. I've always respected the laws of every country I've lived in. I might as well tell you: I've asked to be naturalized French.''

"After being naturalized American?''

"That was a mistake. I don't like the climate over there. I'm sure your friend here understands me.''

He fixed his eyes on Lognon with savage irony, and Lognon blew his nose, not knowing where to look.

"Waiter,'' Maigret called.

"But I told you that you are my guest.''

"Sorry, but I don't accept.''

"I consider that an affront.''

"Have it your own way. Waiter! Bring me the check.''

Maigret was not really as angry as he seemed. Pozzo was tough, and Maigret didn't mind that. And he didn't mind having these top racketeers to deal with either, knowing they had proved too much for the American police. Ruthless, they played to win and stopped at nothing. Hadn't MacDonald said that Cinaglia was a killer? He wouldn't mind being able to telephone Washington in a few days and remark casually, "Hello, Jimmy . . . I got them!''

Maigret hadn't the least idea of the identity of the man who had been tossed out onto the sidewalk of Rue Fléchier almost at Inspector Lognon's feet. He didn't even know if the man was dead or not.

As for the second car, which had picked up the corpse, or the wounded man, it was still more anonymous.

There were two opposing groups in this business as far as he could judge. In the first group there were at least Charlie Cinaglia, Tony Cicero, and Bill Larner, who had hired the car and ransacked Lognon's papers.

But who were the occupants of the second car? Why had they taken the risk of making off with the body?

If the man was dead, what had they done with the corpse?

If not, where was he being cared for?

It was one of the rare investigations in which, at the outset, there was no clue. These people had apparently crossed the Atlantic to settle some scores about which the French police knew nothing.

Their only hope of finding a lead was Pozzo's bar, with its New York atmosphere, so oddly transplanted a stone's throw from the Arc de Triomphe.

"I hope someday I'll get even with you for that!" grumbled the Italian after Maigret had paid the waiter and stood up to go.

"By that you mean?"

"I mean, Superintendent, that I am sure one of these days you will allow me to offer you a good dinner without insulting me by taking out your wallet."

His big mouth was smiling, but his eyes were not. He accompanied the two men to the door and took a malicious pleasure in giving Lognon a friendly pat on the back.

"Shall I call you a taxi?"

"Don't bother."

"Ah, yes, it isn't raining. Well, then, good night, Superintendent. I hope this gentleman will get over the loss of his wife."

The door finally closed, and the policemen began walking down the street. Lognon said nothing. Perhaps he was secretly jubilant to have seen Maigret treated as a novice.

"I've had their wire tapped," the Superintendent told him as they were nearing the corner.

"I thought as much."

Maigret frowned. If Lognon, seeing him go to the telephone, had had that idea, it was all the more certain to have occurred to a man like Pozzo.

"In that case, he won't telephone. He is more likely to send a message."

The street was deserted. A garage on the other side was closed. Avenue MacMahon shone darkly, still wet from the rain, and there was nothing in sight but a cruising taxi and two or three vague forms up toward Avenue de la Grande-Armée.

"I think, Lognon, you'd do well to watch the premises. Since you haven't had much sleep the last few days, I'll send someone to relieve you in a little while."

"I am on night duty all this week."

"But you're supposed to have slept during the day and you haven't."

"That doesn't matter."

Always just as exasperating! Maigret had to exercise a fund of patience he would not have shown toward Janvier or Lucas or any of his own inspectors.

"As soon as someone comes, you go home and to bed."

"If that's an order . . ."

"It's an order. In case you should have to leave before, try your best to phone the Quai."

"Very well, Superintendent."

Maigret left him on the corner and walked quickly to Avenue des Ternes, where he went into a bar and made a telephone call.

"Janvier? Nothing from the switchboard? Good. Who's with you? Torrence? Will you ask him to jump into a taxi and go to Rue des Acacias. He'll find Lognon on watch and he is to relieve him. Lognon will give him the story."

He went home in a taxi, and sat chatting with his wife over a little glass of prunelle.

"Madame Lognon telephoned."

"What about?"

"She hasn't heard from her husband since early in the afternoon and is worried. He was out of sorts, it seems."

He shrugged his shoulders, was on the point of telephoning. No! He'd had enough. He went to bed, slept, was wakened by the smell of coffee, and all the time he was dressing he couldn't get Lognon out of his mind.

When he arrived at the Quai des Orfèvres at nine o'clock, Lucas had replaced Janvier, who had gone home to bed.

"No news from Torrence?"

"He phoned in about ten o'clock last night. Seems he didn't find Lognon on Rue des Acacias."

"Where is he?"

"Torrence? Still there. He just called to ask if he was to keep watching the place. I told him to call back in a few minutes."

Maigret called Lognon's apartment.

"This is Superintendent Maigret."

"Have you heard from my husband? I haven't slept a wink all night. . . ."

"He isn't at home?"

"What! You don't know where he is?"

"And you?"

It was ridiculous. Now he had to reassure her, tell her something, anything at all.

Lognon had disappeared between the time Maigret left him at the corner of Rue des Acacias and the time Torrence arrived to relieve him.

He hadn't telephoned, hadn't given any sign of life.

"Admit, Superintendent, that you agree with me that something terrible must have happened to him. . . . I've always said it would end like this. . . . And I'm all alone, helpless, up here on my fifth floor and can't even move! . . ."

God knows what he said to calm her. By the time he'd finished, he was completely disgusted.

Three

Furious, his hands in his overcoat pockets and stamping his feet, Maigret was waiting, trying to look in over the checked curtains to see what was going on at the back of the restaurant. He had been surprised to find Pozzo's closed. Yet there was a light inside, a single bulb burning at the back of the room.

He had knocked on the window twice, three times, and it seemed to him someone had moved. It wasn't raining this morning. It was very cold, with frost in the air, and the sky was the color of lead. The world seemed hard and wicked.

"He's there," the vegetable man next door told him. "But I'd be surprised if he let you in. He always cleans the place mornings and he doesn't like to be disturbed. He won't open to anyone until eleven, unless you know how to knock."

Maigret tried again and stood on tiptoe so that his face would show above the curtains. He was in no mood to be trifled with this morning. No one could touch one of his men. Even if it was only an inspector of the Ninth Arrondissement, even if it was Lognon.

A dark silhouette, looking, from a distance, somewhat like a bear, finally began to move toward him in the dim light, growing more distinct as it neared the door, and soon Maigret saw Pozzo's face close to his own on the other side of the glass. Only then did the Italian undo a chain, turn a key, and pull open the door.

"Come in," he said, as if he'd been expecting Maigret.

He was wearing a pair of old trousers, baggy in the seat, a pale blue shirt with the sleeves rolled up, and worn red slippers that made him shuffle as he walked. Paying no attention to Maigret, he went back to the rear of the room, where a light was burning and sat down again in front of the remains of a hearty breakfast.

"Make yourself at home. Would you like a cup of coffee?"

"No."

"A little glass of something?"

"No, again."

Without showing surprise, Pozzo shook his head, as much to say, "That's all right. No hard feelings!"

His face was a little gray, and there were bags under his eyes. In fact, he looked not so much like a clown as like certain old comics whose faces are like rubber from grimacing all their lives. And from knocking around the world, they also acquire the same rather vague look of supreme indifference.

In the corner, near the wall, were mops and a bucket. From the kitchen, which could be seen through the service window, came the odor of bacon.

"I thought you were married and that you had children."

And Pozzo, as if playing a scene in slow motion, scratched his head, went to get a cigar from a box on the shelf, lighted it, and blew the smoke almost in Maigret's face.

"Does *your* wife live at the Quai des Orfèvres?" he said finally.

"You live here, don't you?"

"I might answer that it is none of your business. I might even throw you out of my place, and you'd have nothing to complain about. You agree with me? Last night I received you cordially and I tried to invite you to dinner. Not that I like cops. And I don't mean any offense by that, either. But you are somebody in your business, and I respect people who are somebody in their own line. Right! You refused to be my guest. That's your own affair. This morning you disturb me to ask me questions. I can choose either to answer or not to answer.''

''Would you rather I take you down to the PJ?''

''That's something else again, and I'd be curious to see what would happen. You forget that I'm still an American citizen. Before I went with you, I'd take good care to get in touch with my consul.''

He had sat down in front of his empty plate, his elbows on the table, like a man in his own home, and he watched Maigret through the smoke of his cigar.

''You see, Monsieur Maigret, you've been spoiled. After you left last night, someone reminded me that you'd been to America. I could hardly believe it. I wonder what your colleagues over there could have shown you. They must at least have told you that things don't happen the same as here. Just remember I'm in my own home. You understand that word? Suppose someone comes to your apartment and begins asking your wife questions . . . Right. That's just so you'll know who you're dealing with, so you'll damn well know that if I answer your questions, it's because I choose to. No use threatening, like you did last night, to take away my license.

''Now, to get back to your question, I haven't any reason to hide from you that my wife and children live in the country because this is no place for them, and that most of the time I sleep in a room upstairs, and, finally, that in the morning I do my own cleaning up.''

''How did you warn Charlie and Larner?''

''What?''

''Yesterday, after I left, you got word to Charlie and his friends that I'd been here.''

''Really?''

''You didn't telephone.''

''I take it you had my wire tapped.''

"Where is Charlie?"

Pozzo sighed, looked over at the photograph of Cinaglia as a boxer.

"Yesterday," Maigret went on, "I warned you that this was serious. It is even more so today. The Inspector who was with me yesterday has disappeared."

"The cheerful guy?"

"I left him at the corner of the street. Half an hour later, he was no longer there, and he hasn't shown up since. You understand what that means?"

"Should I?"

Maigret managed to restrain himself, but he, too, had become hard, and his eyes never left Pozzo's face.

"I want to know how you warned them. I want to know where they are hiding. Bill Larner hasn't been near the Hotel Wagram. The other two are holed up somewhere, very likely in Paris, and more than likely not far from here, since you were able to get a message to them in a few minutes, without using the phone. You'd better come clean, Pozzo. What time does the waiter get here?"

"At noon."

"And the cook?"

"Three o'clock. We're not open for lunch."

"They'll both be questioned."

"That's your job, isn't it?"

"Where's Charlie?"

Pozzo seemed to be thinking. He rose slowly, as if reluctantly, walked over to the photograph of the boxer, and studied it carefully.

"While you were in the United States, did you go to Chicago, to Detroit, to St. Louis?"

"I went all over the Middle West."

"You probably noticed that the guys over there aren't exactly boy scouts? Was it before or after prohibition?"

"After."

"Well, then, I'm telling you, during prohibition it was ten times, twenty times worse."

Maigret waited, not knowing just what Pozzo was driving at.

"I worked five years as headwaiter in Chicago before I went into business for myself in St. Louis. I opened a restaurant a little like this one, where all sorts of people came—politicians, boxers, gangsters, and artists. And let me tell you, Monsieur Maigret, I never had any trouble with anybody, not even with the police lieutenant who used to come and drink his double whisky at my bar. Do you want to know why?"

He was like an old actor playing to the gallery.

"Because I never stuck my nose into other people's business. Why should I change my rule now that I'm in Paris? Wasn't your spaghetti good? That is something I'm ready to discuss with you."

"But you refuse to tell me where Charlie is?"

"Listen, Maigret . . ."

In another minute he'd be calling him Jules. His tone was almost patronizing, and he was within an ace of putting his hand on Maigret's shoulder.

"In Paris, you're by way of being a great man, and people say you're always the winner. Do you want me to tell you why?"

"What I want is Charlie's address."

"Forget it. We're talking about serious things. You always win because you have nothing but amateurs to deal with. Over there, there aren't any amateurs. And even with the third degree, the police can't often get a guy to talk if he's decided not to."

"Charlie's a killer."

"Really? I suppose the FBI told you that. And did the FBI also tell you why, in that case, they haven't sent Charlie to the electric chair yet?"

Maigret had decided to let him talk, and several times he even forgot to listen as he looked around the room with a scowl on his face. He was pursuing his idea. Charlie and his friends had certainly been warned that Maigret and

Lognon were at Pozzo's. The telephone hadn't been used. If someone had left the restaurant to warn them, that someone hadn't gone very far. On the other hand, if Lognon had seen the waiter leave, for example, or the cook, or Pozzo himself, he would have been suspicious.

"And that's where all the difference lies, Maigret, the difference between amateurs and professionals. Didn't I just tell you that I respect anyone who is somebody in his line?"

"Including killers?"

"Yesterday you told me a story that's none of my business and that I've already forgotten. This morning you come here and give me some more of the same, and I'm not having any. You're a real man, and probably a good guy, too. You enjoy a fine reputation. I don't know if the gentlemen of the FBI asked you to take charge of this business, but I doubt it. So now I'm telling you: 'Drop it!' "

"Thanks for the advice."

"It's sincere. When Charlie was fighting in Chicago, he was in the featherweight class, and it never entered his head to take on a heavyweight."

"When did you see him lately?"

Pozzo, with a sort of ostentation, remained silent.

"I suppose you couldn't tell me the name of the customers you were shooting craps with, either?"

Pozzo's face showed amazement.

"Am I supposed to know the name, the address, and the family history of all my customers?"

Like Pozzo a few moments before, Maigret got up and, with the same absent air, walked over behind the bar and examined the shelves under it.

Pozzo watched him with apparent indifference.

"You see, when I find one of those customers, I have an idea things will begin to get a little hot for you."

Maigret held up a pad and pencil he'd just found.

"I know now how you warned Charlie, or Bill Larner,

or Cicero; it doesn't matter which, since they're working together. My mistake was thinking it was after I left. But it happened while I was still here. When you saw me come in with the Inspector, you knew what was up. You had time while we were ordering dinner to scribble a message on the pad and slip it to one of those two customers at the bar. What do you say to that?''

"I say it's extremely interesting."

"That's all?"

"That's all."

The telephone rang in the booth. Pozzo scowled but went to answer it.

"It's for you!" he said.

Maigret had left word where he was going, and it was Lucas on the wire.

"They've found him, Chief."

There was something in Lucas's voice that told Maigret that things had taken an unpleasant turn.

"Dead?"

"No. About an hour ago, a fish dealer from Honfleur driving along Route 13 in the Forest of Saint-Germain between Poissy and Le Pecq picked up a man lying unconscious at the side of the road."

"Lognon?"

"Yes. He seemed in a bad way. The dealer took him to Dr. Grenier's in Saint-Germain, and the doctor's just phoned us."

"Wounded?"

"The face is all swollen, probably smashed by somebody's fists, but there's a wound in his head that's more serious. According to the doctor, he must have been hit hard with the butt of a revolver. Anyway, I thought I'd better get an ambulance and have him taken to Beaujon right away. He'll be there in another fifteen minutes."

"Anything else?"

"Through the boardinghouses we've picked up the trail of the two men."

"Charlie and Cicero?"

"Yes. Ten days ago they arrived in Paris from Le Havre and went to the Hotel de l'Etoile, Rue Brey. They were out all night Monday. Tuesday morning they came back, paid their bill, and left with their luggage."

It all centered around the same neighborhood: Rue Brey, Hotel Wagram, Pozzo's restaurant, Rue des Acacias, the garage where the automobile had been rented.

"That's all?"

"An automobile that was stolen last night about nine o'clock on Avenue de la Grande-Armée was found this morning at the Porte Maillot. It belongs to an engineer who was playing bridge at some friend's. He states that he'd had his car washed yesterday afternoon, but it was found covered with mud, as if it had been driven along country roads."

Still the same neighborhood.

"What do you want me to do, Chief?"

"Go to Beaujon and wait for me."

"Shall I notify Madame Lognon?"

Maigret heaved a sigh.

"You'd better, of course. Don't give her any details. Tell her he isn't dead. And I don't think you ought to do it by phone. You could run up to Place Constantin-Pecqueur before going to Beaujon."

"That'll certainly be a picnic!"

"Don't mention his being beaten up."

"All right."

Maigret almost smiled. It really seemed that for once luck was with the lugubrious Lognon. If he was seriously hurt, he would become a sort of hero, probably receive a medal!

"I'll be seeing you, Chief!"

"Good luck."

Pozzo, meantime, had begun sweeping out his restaurant, with the chairs piled up on the tables.

"My inspector was beaten up," Maigret told him, looking him straight in the eye.

But he didn't get any reaction.

"Only beaten up?"

"That surprises you?"

"Not much. It's probably a warning. That's done a lot over there."

"You still refuse to open up?"

"I've told you I never poke my nose into other people's business."

"You'll see me again."

"That will be a pleasure."

Just as he was about to go out, Maigret turned on his heel and went back to get the pad he had left on the table. This time he caught a look of uneasiness on Pozzo's face.

"Hey! That's mine."

"I'll return it."

He found the police car waiting for him.

"Beaujon," he said.

Then, when they were in front of the dark entrance of the hospital, he gave the pad to the policeman who was driving.

"You're to go back to the Quai. Take this up to the laboratory and give it to Moers. Careful how you handle it."

"What shall I tell him?"

"Nothing. He'll know what it's about."

Thinking he had plenty of time before the ambulance arrived, he went into a bar, ordered a Calvados, and shut himself in the telephone booth.

"Moers? Maigret speaking. I've sent you a pad of paper. Last night I think someone wrote something on one of the sheets and tore it off."

"I see. You want to find out if it left an imprint on the next sheet?"

"That's it. It's possible the pad hasn't been used since,

but I'm not sure. And make it fast. I'll be at the office about noon.''

''Understood, Chief.''

As a matter of fact, Pozzo's calm assurance had not left Maigret unimpressed. There was a grain of truth, and even more than a grain, in what the restaurateur had said. It was the general opinion in the Crime Squad that most, if not all, murderers were imbeciles.

''Amateurs!'' Pozzo had declared.

He wasn't far wrong. On the east side of the Atlantic barely ten percent escaped the police, whereas over on the other side known killers like Cinaglia were free to go where they pleased for lack of evidence against them.

They were professionals, to use Pozzo's language, who played to win and stopped at nothing.

The Superintendent couldn't remember anyone ever having talked to him in that patronizing tone before: ''Drop it!''

Naturally, he didn't intend to do any such thing, but he couldn't help thinking that yesterday on the phone Mac-Donald had not exactly encouraged him.

He wasn't on familiar ground. He was confronted by people whose methods he didn't know, except by hearsay, and whose mentality and reactions were a mystery to him.

Why had Charlie and Tony Cicero come to Paris? They seemed to have crossed the ocean with a definite purpose in mind, and they had lost no time.

Eight days after their arrival, they left a body on the sidewalk near the Church of Notre-Dame-de-Lorette.

That body, alive or dead, had disappeared a few minutes later, almost under Lognon's nose.

''The same.''

He drank a second Calvados, with the feeling that he really was catching cold. Then he crossed the street and arrived at the hospital just as an ambulance drove up.

It was Lognon, being brought from Saint-Germain. He was insisting that he could walk. When he caught sight of

Maigret, they could no longer hold him down on the stretcher.

"But I tell you I'm perfectly able to stand up."

For a moment Maigret had to turn his face away. In spite of everything, he couldn't help smiling at the sight of Old Grouch. One eye was swollen and completely closed, and the doctor at Saint-Germain had covered a corner of his mouth and the side of one nostril with gaudy pink adhesive tape.

"Superintendent, I must explain . . ."

"Later . . ."

Poor Lognon staggered, and a nurse had to help him to the room that had been prepared for him. An intern accompanied them.

"Call me as soon as you've fixed him up. Try to get him in shape to talk."

Maigret walked up and down the corridor, and ten minutes later Lucas joined him.

"And Madame Lognon? Pretty grim?"

Lucas's expression was eloquent.

"She was indignant because he hadn't been brought home. She insists that they have no right to keep him in the hospital, away from her."

"How would she take care of him?"

"That's what I pointed out to her. She wants to see you, talks of calling the Commissioner. According to her, she's being neglected, left there alone, sick and unprotected, at the mercy of gangsters."

"You told her we had a man watching the building?"

"Yes. That calmed her down a little. I had to take her over to the window and show her the man on duty outside. At the end she said, 'Some people get the honors, others all the raw deals.' "

When the intern came out of the room, he seemed worried.

"Fracture of the skull?" asked Maigret in a low voice.

"I don't think so. We'll get an X-ray later, but it's unlikely. Only, he's taken an awful beating. Besides, he's been out in the forest all night, and there's a chance of pneumonia. You can talk to him. It'll relieve his mind. He keeps asking for you, refuses to let us do a thing before he sees you. I had the devil of a time getting him to let me give him a shot of penicillin, he was so afraid I wanted to put him to sleep. I had to show him the name on the ampoule.''

''Better if I see him alone,'' Maigret said to Lucas.

Lognon was lying in a white bed, with a nurse fussing around the room. His face was now very flushed, as if his temperature was rising.

Maigret sat down beside the bed.

''Well, old man?''

''They got me.''

A tear appeared in his one good eye.

''The doctor says you mustn't excite yourself. Just give me the essentials.''

''When you left me, I stayed at the corner, where I could watch the door of the restaurant. I stood flat against the wall quite a distance from the streetlight.''

''No one left Pozzo's?''

''No one. In about ten minutes, a car came down Avenue MacMahon, made the turn, and stopped right in front of me.''

''Charlie Cinaglia?''

''There were three of them. It was Cicero, the big one, who was driving, with Bill Larner beside him. Charlie was in the back. I didn't even have time to take my revolver from my pocket. Charlie had the door open already and his automatic aimed at me. He didn't say anything, just motioned me to get in. The two others didn't even look around. What should I have done?''

''Climbed in,'' sighed Maigret.

''The car started off right away, while my pockets were felt and my gun taken away. No one spoke. I saw we were leaving Paris by the Porte Maillot; then I recognized the Saint-Germain road.''

"The car stopped in the forest?''

"Yes. It was Larner who kept directing his friend at the wheel. We went down a little side road and stopped a long way from the highway. They made me get out.''

Hadn't Pozzo been right in his contention that they weren't amateurs?

"Charlie never opened his mouth. It was the big one, Cicero, with his hands in his pockets and smoking one cigarette after another, who told Larner, in English, what questions to ask me.''

"In other words, they'd taken Larner along as interpreter?''

"Yes. And I don't think he was happy about his job. Several times he seemed to be advising them to let up on me. Before they began asking questions, Charlie had smashed his fist right in my face, and my nose started bleeding.

" 'I think you'd better be nice,' Larner said, with a slight accent, 'and tell these gentlemen what they want to know.'

"It was really always the same question they asked:

" 'What have you done with the body?'

"At first I didn't want to give them the satisfaction of answering, and just glowered at them. Then Cicero said something to Charlie in English, and he hit me again.

" 'You're making a mistake,' Larner said, and he looked annoyed. 'People always talk in the end, you know.'

"After four or five more punches—I don't remember how many—I swore that I didn't know what had happened to the body, that I didn't even know who it was.

"They didn't believe me. Cicero kept on smoking, and he'd walk around now and then to stretch his legs.

" 'Who told the police?'

"What was I to say? That I just happened to be there, not because of them, but on another job entirely?

"Every time I answered, Cicero would motion to Charlie, who was just waiting to punch me in the face again.

"They emptied my pockets, examined my wallet under the automobile headlights."

"How long did it last?"

"I don't know. Maybe half an hour, maybe longer. I hurt all over. One blow had cut my eye, and I could feel the blood running down my face.

" 'I swear I don't know a thing,' I told them.

"Cicero wasn't satisfied and began talking to Larner again. Larner asked me more questions. He asked me if I'd seen another car stop on Rue Fléchier. I said I had.

" 'What was the license number?'

" 'I didn't have time to see the number.'

" 'You're lying!'

" 'I'm not lying.'

"They'd seen you go into my place and wanted to know who you were. I told them. Then they asked me if you'd been in touch with the FBI and I said I didn't know, that in France inspectors didn't ask superintendents questions. Larner laughed at that. He seemed to know you.

"Finally, Cicero shrugged his shoulders and walked off toward the car. Larner, looking relieved, followed him, but Charlie stayed behind. He shouted something after them. I don't think they answered. Then he pulled his automatic from his pocket, and I thought he was going to kill me. I . . ."

Lognon was suddenly silent; tears of rage shone in his one eye. Maigret preferred not to know what he had done—if he'd fallen on his knees, if he'd pleaded. Probably not. Lognon was capable of just standing there, glowering and bitter to the end.

"But he only hit me over the head with the butt of the gun, and I lost consciousness.

"When I came to, they'd gone. I tried to get up. I shouted for help."

"You roamed around the forest all night?"

"I must have turned in circles. I passed out several times. Sometimes I'd crawl on my hands and knees. I'd hear automobiles passing and I'd do my best to shout. In the morning, I found myself at the edge of the highway, and a truck stopped and picked me up."

Without transition he asked:

"Has my wife been notified?"

"Yes. Lucas went to see her."

"What did she say?"

"She insisted on your being brought home."

A look of distress appeared in Lognon's one eye.

"They're going to take me home?"

"No. You need medical care, and you'll be better off here."

"I did the best I could."

"Of course you did."

Then it was as though Lognon was suddenly struck by a thought that worried him. He hesitated, finally muttering as he looked away:

"I'm not worthy to be in the police."

"Why?"

"Because, if I'd known where the body was, I'd have ended up by telling them."

"So would I," Maigret rejoined, without its being quite clear if he just said it to make the Inspector happy.

"Will I have to stay in the hospital long?"

"A few days at least."

"And I won't be told what's happening?"

"Of course you will."

"You promise? You're not angry with me?"

"What for, old man?"

"You know very well it's my fault."

He was really taking advantage of the situation. Of course Maigret had to deny it, had to repeat that he had done his duty, that if he hadn't acted as he had Monday night, they might never have got on the track of Charlie and Cicero.

Besides, it was almost true.

"What is my wife doing about the marketing?"

Maigret replied at random:

"Lucas is taking care of it."

"I'm ashamed to be giving you all this trouble."

That was Lognon. He hadn't changed. Exaggerated humility. He couldn't help exaggerating, one way or the other. Fortunately, someone knocked at the door just then, for Maigret didn't know how to make his escape. The nurse announced:

"It's time to go for the X-ray."

This time Lognon was forced to lie down on the wheeled stretcher, and when he passed by, Lucas, who was waiting in the corridor, gave him a friendly nod.

"Let's go."

"What did they do to him?"

Without replying directly, Maigret murmured:

"Pozzo's right. They're tough."

Then, thoughtfully:

"What amazes me is that a man like Bill Larner should be working with them. Swindlers in his class aren't in the habit of taking chances."

"You think the other two forced him to help them?"

"At any rate, I'd like to have a little talk with him."

Larner was also a professional, but of a different kind, a different class, one of those international crooks who pull off a job only once in a long while, a really serious job, carefully planned down to the last detail, that nets them twenty or thirty thousand dollars, and afterward allows them to rest on their laurels, as it were, unnoticed. He had been in Paris for two years now, and during that time he had apparently been living on his capital and had not once been bothered.

Maigret and Lucas took a taxi, and the Superintendent

gave the address of police headquarters. Then, as they were crossing Rue Royale, he changed his mind.

"Rue des Capucines," he told the driver. "Manhattan Bar."

The idea had come to him while he was thinking of the photographs at Pozzo's. At the Manhattan, too, the walls were decorated with photographs of boxers and actors. But it wasn't the same clientele as at Rue des Acacias. For twenty years, Luigi had seen the whole American colony and the pick of the tourists from across the Atlantic file through. It was not yet noon, and the place was almost deserted. Luigi himself was behind the bar, arranging his bottles.

"Greetings, Superintendent. What can I offer you?"

Like Pozzo, he was of Italian origin, and it was said that all the money he made in his restaurant he lost at the races. By betting not only on the horses, but on anything and everything. Boxing matches, tennis tournaments, swimming meets—everything served as an excuse for betting, including tomorrow's weather.

During the slack hours of the afternoon, between three and five, with a compatriot who was vaguely connected with the embassy, he would often bet on the automobiles streaming past the windows.

"I bet you five thousand francs that twenty Citroëns go by within ten minutes."

"It's a bet."

For the sake of the local color, Maigret ordered a whisky and, letting his eyes wander over the rows of pictures on the walls, was not long in locating one of Charlie Cinaglia in boxing trunks, exactly the same photograph he had seen at Pozzo's, except that this one was not signed.

Four

When the two of them left the Manhattan Bar in their black overcoats and black hats, with Maigret looking twice as tall and broad as Lucas, they were for all the world like two widowers who had stopped at several bars on their way home from the cemetery.

Had Luigi done it intentionally? It was possible. In any case, he had not done it maliciously. He was a decent man, no one had anything to say against him, and the most notable personalities at the U.S. Embassy were not ashamed of lingering at his bar.

He had been generous with his drinks, that's all, especially to Maigret, and it had been a long time since the Superintendent had tasted whisky. Besides, he had just had two glasses of Calvados on Faubourg Saint-Honoré.

He wasn't drunk, and neither was Lucas. Did Lucas think his chief was? He had an odd way of glancing up at him as they threaded their way through the crowd.

Lucas had not been at Pozzo's that morning. He hadn't heard Pozzo's speech or, rather, his lecture, and consequently it was difficult for him to understand Maigret's state of mind.

First of all, and almost at once, there had been Luigi's little lecture on boxers. Maigret had looked at Charlie's picture and had asked casually, as if it didn't matter one way or the other:

"You know him?"

"A little guy who might have gone a long way. He was

probably the best in his class, and he'd worked hard to get there. Then one fine day he gets himself mixed up in some shady business, and he's not allowed to fight any more.''

''What happened to him?''

''What do you think happens to boys like that? Every year thousands of them, in Chicago, in Detroit, in New York, in all the big cities, enroll in training gyms, sure they're going to be champions. But how many champions can you count in a generation, Superintendent?''

''I don't know. Not many, naturally.''

''And even for them, success doesn't last long. Those who haven't spent their money on platinum blonds and Cadillacs open a restaurant or a sporting-goods shop. But what about the rest, all the youngsters who thought they'd arrived and who end up punch-drunk from being hit in the head so much? They've learned how to hit and nothing else. But there are always people who need them as body-guards, as strong-arm men. That's what happened to Charlie.''

''I've heard he's become a killer.''

Then Luigi said, as though it were the most natural thing in the world:

''It's possible.''

''You haven't seen him lately?''

Maigret had asked the question with his most innocent air, not even looking at Luigi. He knew Luigi, and Luigi knew him. The two men appreciated each other. And now, in a flash, the atmosphere was no longer the same.

''Is he in Paris?''

''I think so.''

''How do you happen to be interested in him?''

''Oh, just incidentally . . .''

''I've never seen Charlie Cinaglia in the flesh. I left the United States before he'd made a name for himself. I hadn't heard he'd come to Europe.''

''I thought someone might have spoken to you about

him. He's been to Pozzo's several times. And, since both of you are of Italian origin . . ."

"I am of Neapolitan origin," Luigi corrected him.

"And Pozzo?"

"Sicilian. It's as if you'd confused a Corsican with someone from Marseilles."

"I wonder who else, beside Pozzo, Charlie went to see on arriving in Paris. He didn't come alone. Tony Cicero was with him."

That was when Luigi filled his glass a second time. Maigret seemed a little vague, spoke lifelessly, without conviction. It was what Lucas, who knew him well, called "going fishing," and Maigret sometime succeeded in appearing so perfectly innocuous that he even fooled his collaborators.

"It all seems extremely complicated." He sighed. "To say nothing of another American in this business, Bill Larner."

"Bill has nothing in common with the other two," Luigi protested quickly. "Bill is a gentleman."

"One of your customers?"

"He comes here from time to time."

"Suppose Bill Larner had to hide out. Where do you think he'd go?"

"Suppose, as you say, since I don't believe that could ever happen—Bill would hide out where nobody would find him. But you can take it from me, Bill has nothing in common with the other two."

"You know Cicero?"

"Sometimes his name appears in the American papers."

"A gangster?"

"Are you seriously interested in these people?"

Luigi had lost some of his cordiality. In spite of his insistence that he was a Neapolitan and not a Sicilian, he now began speaking and looking at the Superintendent a little like Pozzo had.

"You've been to the United States, haven't you? Then you ought to realize that these aren't matters for the French police. The Americans themselves, with the exception of a few FBI agents, can't get anywhere with these organizations. I don't know what the individuals you're talking about are doing in Paris—that is, if they are in Paris. If you say they are, I'll accept it, but it's news to me. In any case, what they're up to is no concern of ours."

"And if they've killed a man?"

"A Frenchman?"

"I don't know."

"If they killed someone, it's because they were ordered to do the job, and you'll never get evidence against them to prove it. Let me point out that I know neither of them. The two you first mentioned are Sicilians. As for Bill Larner, I still insist that he has nothing in common with them."

"In what connection do the American papers speak of Cicero?"

"In connection with rackets, most likely. You can't understand. Here, you don't have any real criminal organizations like the ones over there. You don't even have real killers. Suppose a guy in Paris went around to the shopkeepers in his neighborhood and explained that they were in need of protection against some tough customers and that, for a consideration of so many thousand francs a week, he would do the protecting. The shopkeeper would go right to the police, wouldn't he? Or he would laugh in the man's face. Well, in America nobody laughs, and only fools go to the police. Because if they do, or if they don't pay up, a bomb explodes in their shop, unless they're riddled with machine-gun bullets on their way home."

Luigi was warming to his subject. As with Pozzo, you would have sworn that he was proud of his compatriots.

"That isn't all. Suppose one of these characters is arrested. There's almost always a judge or a powerful politician to get him off. Or let's say the sheriff or the district attorney gets stubborn. A dozen witnesses will come for-

ward to testify that the poor guy was at the other end of
town at the time. And if an honest witness claims the
opposite, and if he's crazy enough to stick to it, he'll have
an accident before the day of the trial. You get me?''

A tall blond man had just come in and was leaning on
the bar a few feet from Maigret and Lucas. Luigi gave
him a wink.

"A martini?"

"A martini," the newcomer repeated, looking at the
two Frenchmen with an expression of amusement.

Maigret had already blown his nose once or twice. It
tickled. His eyelids felt hot. Had he caught Lognon's cold?

Lucas, good old Lucas, was waiting for some reaction
on Maigret's part. But the Superintendent let Luigi go on
talking as if he had nothing to reply.

To tell the truth, he was beginning to get fed up. That
Pozzo should tell him to drop it was one thing. The restaurateur on Rue des Acacias probably had his reasons.

But that here in this fashionable bar a Luigi should tell
him the same thing was just a little too much.

"Suppose, Superintendent, that an American arrived in
Marseilles, and tried to get nosy about the tough boys
down there. You know damn well what would happen to
him! Well, let me tell you, they're mere children compared
to . . .''

Yes, yes! Who knows? Perhaps if Maigret had gone to
the U.S. consul or the ambassador, those gentlemen would
have said the same thing: "Keep out of it, Maigret. This
is not for you.''

Not for the kindergarten, in other words! He almost felt
like answering, which of course would have been ridiculous: ''And Landru? Was that kindergarten stuff too?''

Silent and sullen, he had drained his glass, feeling certain that Lucas was disappointed in him and was wondering why he didn't put Luigi in his place.

Now that they were out on the street, Lucas still didn't
dare ask any questions. Maigret said nothing about taking

a taxi or a bus. He was walking along sulkily, his hands in his pockets, and they had gone some distance when, turning to Lucas, he said very seriously:

"What do you want to bet I'll get them?"

"I'm sure of it," Lucas made haste to reply.

"I am positive! Understand? Positive! They give me a——!"

Maigret didn't often indulge in offensive expressions, but he gave vent to this one with a feeling of relief.

Nothing might come of it, but, on the off chance, he had sent Lucas to Rue des Acacias to keep an eye on Pozzo's restaurant.

"No use trying to keep under cover. Our friend is smart enough to spot you. I'm pretty sure he hasn't telephoned, because he knows his line's tapped, but he must have got word to those two fellows who were at the bar yesterday to warn Charlie and Cicero. There is just a chance they couldn't contact them and that one of them may come back to Rue des Acacias."

He had described them to Lucas, had given him detailed instructions. Back at the Quai des Orfèvres, he went straight to the laboratory without stopping at his office.

Moers was eating a sandwich while waiting for him. He at once turned on a projector, which looked like a huge magic lantern, and an image appeared on the screen.

It showed the marks Pozzo's pencil had left on the pad. The first characters were fairly distinct: G A L. After that came some numbers.

"As you thought, Chief, it's a telephone number. The exchange is Galvani. The first number is a 2, the second a 7, the third is completely illegible, the fourth too, perhaps a zero, but I'm not sure, or a 9 or a 6."

Moers, too, was looking at him curiously, not because Maigret smelled of whisky, but because of a peculiar air of vagueness about him. In addition, when he was leaving, he used a word he never said except at moments like this:

"Thanks, *son!*"

He went to his office, took off his overcoat, and opened the door to the inspectors' office.

"Janvier, Lapointe . . ."

Before giving them instructions, he phoned the Brasserie Dauphine.

"Have you eaten, you two?"

"Yes, Chief."

He ordered sandwiches for himself and beer for all of them.

"Each of you take a list of telephone numbers. Look under Galvani."

It was a tremendous job. Without an extraordinary stroke of luck, it would take them hours to find the right number.

Yesterday, the two men at Pozzo's had gone out just after the waiter brought the spaghetti—in other words, about three-quarters of an hour to an hour before Maigret and Lognon left. Pozzo had told them to phone a certain number with a Galvani exchange. That was in the Avenue de la Grande-Armée zone. And wasn't it on Avenue de la Grande-Armée that the car which had taken Lognon to the Forest of Saint-Germain had been stolen?

It all added up. Either the three Americans were together when they had been notified, or else they were able to get together very quickly. In fact, an hour later they were on the lookout near the restaurant.

"Would it be a hotel, Chief?"

"I have no idea. Perhaps. At any rate, they haven't registered at any hotel under their real names. If they're at a hotel, they must have got hold of false identification cards or passports."

That wasn't impossible. A man like Pozzo must know the ropes.

"But I don't think they're at a hotel or a boardinghouse. They know that's where we'd be apt to look first."

At one of Larner's friends', perhaps, since Larner had

been living in Paris for two years and must have connections. In that case, it was probably at a woman's.

"Try all the numbers that seem to fit. Draw up a list of women living alone, with American and Italian names."

He had no illusions. When they hit on the right number, if they did, the birds would have flown. Pozzo was neither a simpleton nor a novice. He had seen Maigret put the pad in his pocket. By this time, he had once more given the alarm.

Maigret telephoned his wife that he would not be home for lunch. Then he called Madame Lognon, who complained some more.

The door between his office and that of the inspectors was still open. He could hear Janvier and Lapointe telephoning various numbers, reciting a different story each time, and little by little he sank deeper into his chair and pulled less and less frequently on his pipe.

But he wasn't asleep. He felt hot. He was almost sure he had a temperature. His eyes half closed, he tried to think, but his mind was getting foggier and foggier, until there was just one thought that kept hammering in his head: I'll get them!

How he was going to "get them" was another matter. To tell the truth, he hadn't the faintest idea, but seldom in his life had he been so determined to accomplish a task. It was almost taking on the proportions of a national issue, and the very word "gangster" was enough to put him in a foul mood.

Precisely, Monsieur Luigi! Precisely, Monsieur Pozzo! Precisely, all you Americans! None of you will make me change my mind. I've always said, and I still say, that murderers are imbeciles. If they weren't, they wouldn't kill. Do you understand? No? You're not convinced? Well, all right. I, Maigret, will prove it. There! That's all. It's settled! . . .

* * *

When the office boy knocked at the door and, getting no answer, peeped in, Maigret was sleeping, with his pipe dangling from his mouth.

"Express letter, Superintendent."

They were the photographs and records sent by air from Washington.

Ten minutes later, the laboratory was busy making a series of photos. At four o'clock, the reporters gathered in the waiting room, and Maigret handed out copies.

"Don't ask me why they are wanted. Just help me find them. Run the pictures on the front page. Say that anyone who has seen one of these men is requested to phone my office immediately."

"Are they armed?"

Maigret hesitated before replying honestly:

"They are not only armed, but also dangerous."

And, using the word that was beginning to irritate him:

"They're killers. At least one of them is."

Their pictures were being telephotoed to all the railway stations, border posts, post offices, and local police.

All this, as poor Lognon would have said, was easy. Lucas was cooling his heels on the corner of Rue des Acacias. Janvier and Lapointe kept on telephoning. As soon as they hit on a number that seemed to them suspicious, they sent someone to verify it.

At five o'clock, Maigret was told that Washington was calling, and he heard the voice of MacDonald hailing him with a cordial "Jules."

"Jules, I've been thinking about your telephone call, and I've had occasion to mention it casually to the big boss. . . ."

Maigret was perhaps imagining things, but it seemed to him that MacDonald sounded less frank than the day before. There were long pauses.

"Yes, I'm listening."

"Are you sure that Cinaglia and Cicero are in Paris?"

"Positive. I've just had it confirmed from their photographs by someone who saw them close up."

It was true. He had sent an inspector up to Madame Lognon, and she had been positive.

"Hello! . . ."

"Yes. I'm still listening."

"Are there only two of them?"

"They have made contact with Bill Larner."

"As I told you before, he's not important. They haven't met anyone else?"

"That's what I'm trying to find out."

MacDonald seemed to be beating about the bush, like someone who was afraid of saying too much.

"You haven't heard anything of a third Sicilian?"

"What's his name?"

Another hesitation.

"Mascarelli."

"Would he have arrived at the same time as the others?"

"Certainly not. Several weeks earlier."

"I'll have the name looked up by our Hotel Squad."

"Mascarelli is not registered under his own name probably."

"In that case . . ."

"Try anyway. If you hear of a Mascarelli, nicknamed Sloppy Joe, let me know, preferably by telephone. Here's his description. Short and skinny, looks fifty and is only forty-one, sickly looking, with scars from boils on his neck. You understand the word 'sloppy'?"

Maigret understood the word, but would have been hard put to translate it into French exactly.

"Good! That's his nickname and he fully deserves it."

"What's he doing in France?"

A silence at the other end of the wire.

"What are the other two doing here?"

MacDonald said something in an undertone, as if conferring with someone standing beside him, then finally replied:

"If Charlie Cinaglia and Cicero met Sloppy Joe in Paris, the chances are that the body your inspector saw thrown out of a car was Sloppy Joe."

"That is very enlightening," rejoined Maigret sarcastically.

"I'm sorry, Jules, but that's about all I know myself."

The Superintendent called Le Havre, then Cherbourg, got hold of the officials in charge of incoming passengers. They examined passenger lists without finding any Mascarelli. Maigret described him as best he could, and they promised to question their inspectors.

Janvier came in.

"Torrence wants you on the phone, Chief."

"Where is he?"

"In the neighborhood of Grande-Armée, verifying addresses."

It was hardly worthwhile for him to come back to the Quai des Orfèvres each time. He telephoned results from a bar, and was given another address.

"Hello! Is that you, Chief? I'm phoning from the apartment of a lady I'd rather keep an eye on. I think you'd better come and have a little talk with her. She is not very agreeable."

Maigret heard a woman's voice in the background, then Torrence's, no longer speaking into the phone:

"If you don't shut up now, I'll smack your face for you. . . . Are you there, Chief? I am at 28 *bis* Rue Brunel, third floor left. The woman's name is Adrienne Laur. It might be a good idea to see if the name's registered."

Maigret entrusted Lapointe with the job, then, putting on his heavy overcoat and picking up two pipes from his desk, he went downstairs. He was lucky enough to find one of the police cars in the courtyard.

"Rue Brunel."

Still the same neighborhood, not far from Avenue Wagram, only a couple of hundred yards from Rue des Acacias, perhaps three hundred from the place where the automobile had been stolen the previous evening. It was a comfortable, middle-class apartment house. There was an elevator, carpeting on the stairs. When he reached the third floor, a door opened, and big Torrence stood there looking relieved.

"Maybe you can get something out of her, Chief. I give up!"

A dark woman with quite opulent curves was standing in the middle of the living room wearing nothing but a housecoat that opened every time she moved.

"What, another!" she greeted him sarcastically. "How many are you going to use against me?"

Politely, Maigret took off his hat and laid it on a chair and, since it was very hot in the room, he also removed his coat, murmuring:

"With your permission."

"I'm not permitting a thing!"

She was really quite good-looking, about thirty, with the husky voice of those who live at night and sleep by day. The room reeked of a heavy perfume. The bedroom door stood open, disclosing an unmade bed, and in the living room there was a bed pillow on the couch, another on the floor, where two rugs had been laid, one on top of the other.

Torrence, who had followed Maigret's glance, said:

"You see the setup, Chief?"

It was evident that she was not the only person who had slept in the apartment the night before.

"She took her own sweet time answering after I rang. She claims she was asleep. She was even sleeping in the raw, because she hasn't a stitch on under that thing."

"And what business is it of yours?"

"I asked her if she knew an American named Bill Larner and I saw she was hesitating, playing for time, pretending to be trying to remember. She tried to stop me from looking in the bedroom. Take a look for yourself. On that chest of drawers to the left."

In a red leather frame, there was a photograph, probably taken at Deauville, of a man and a woman in bathing suits: Adrienne Laur and Bill Larner.

"You see why I telephoned you? That's not all. Just glance at that wastebasket. I counted eight cigar butts. And they are those extra-long Havanas that last at least an hour. I suppose when I rang, she noticed the ashtrays full of butts and dumped them in the basket in a hurry."

"I had friends in yesterday evening."

"How many friends?"

"It's none of your business."

"Bill Larner?"

"That's none of your business either. Besides, that picture was taken a year ago, and since then we've broken up."

There was a bottle of brandy and a glass on the table; she poured herself a drink without offering them any, lighted another cigarette, fluffed up her hair in the back.

"Am I going to be allowed to go back to bed?"

"Listen, my dear . . ."

"I'm not your dear."

"You'd be smart to answer my questions like a good girl."

"Oh, really!"

"You didn't see any harm in it. Larner asked you to let him stay here with two of his friends. He probably didn't explain why."

"I just love the sound of your voice, honey."

Torrence's expression seemed to say, "You see how she is!"

And Maigret, without losing patience:

"Are you French, Adrienne?"

"She's Belgian," Torrence put in. "I saw her identification card in her bag. She was born in Antwerp and has been living in France for five years."

"In other words, we can take away your work permit. I suppose you work in night clubs?"

"She's one of the Folies-Bergère nudes," Torrence again interposed.

"So what? I'm a Folies-Bergère nude. And that gives you the right to barge in here as in a stable, I suppose! You, big boy"—turning on Torrence—"if I hadn't snatched your hat off your head you wouldn't have bothered taking it off. But every time my housecoat opens a little I know very well where you look."

"Listen, Adrienne. I don't know what Larner told you. He probably didn't tell you the truth about his friends. Do you speak English?"

"Plenty for what I do with it."

"The two men who slept here are wanted for murder. You know what that means? It means you can be prosecuted as an accessory after the fact. Do you know how many years you can get for that?"

He had struck home. She had stopped pacing up and down, was looking at him anxiously.

"Five to ten years."

"I haven't done anything."

"I'm sure you haven't, and that's why I'm telling you you're making a mistake. It's fine to help a friend, on condition you don't have to pay too high a price."

"You're trying to make me talk."

"The shorter of the two men Bill brought here with him is called Charlie."

She didn't deny it.

"The other is Tony Cicero."

"I don't know them. I know that Bill never killed anyone."

"I know it too. I am even convinced that Bill wasn't helping them of his own free will."

"Are you serious?"

She looked at the bottle, poured herself another half glass, almost offered one to Maigret, shrugged.

"I've known Larner for years," Maigret said.

"He's only been in France for two years."

"But for fifteen we've had his record in our files. As someone said to me recently, he's a gentleman."

She was watching him, frowning, not too sure whether he wasn't trying to trap her.

"For at least two days, probably three, Charlie and Cicero have been hiding out here. Have you a refrigerator?"

Once more Torrence interrupted:

"I thought of that. There's one in the kitchen. It's full. Two cold chickens, half a ham, almost a whole salami . . ."

"Yesterday evening," Maigret continued, "someone telephoned and delivered a message; then they all left in a hurry."

She sat down now and with unexpected modesty pulled her housecoat over her legs and thighs.

"They came back sometime during the night," he went on. "I'm sure they'd been drinking. Especially Bill Larner, if what I know of him is true, because he had just witnessed a scene that was too much for him."

As Torrence kept roaming around the apartment, she snapped at him:

"Hey, you! Can't you stay quiet a minute?"

Then she turned to Maigret.

"Well, what else?"

"I don't know what time this morning they got another message. Not before eleven o'clock, at any rate. They were probably asleep, Bill in your bed, the other two in this room. They got dressed in a hurry. Did they tell you where they were going?"

"You're trying to drag me into this!"

"On the contrary, I'm trying to pull you out!"

"Are you the Maigret the papers are always talking about?"

"Why do you ask?"

"Because they say you're a regular guy. But I don't like that big bum!"

"What did they say when they left?"

"Nothing. Not even thanks."

"How did Bill seem?"

"I've never admitted Bill was here."

"You must have heard what they said when they were getting ready to leave."

"They were talking English."

"I thought you knew English."

"Not the kind they were talking."

"Last night, when he was alone with you in your room, Bill talked to you about his friends."

"How do you know?"

"Didn't he tell you confidentially that he was going to try to get rid of them?"

"He said that as soon as he could he'd take them out to the country."

"Where?"

"I don't know."

"Did he often go to the country?"

"Practically never."

"Didn't you ever go together?"

"No."

"You were his mistress, weren't you?"

"From time to time."

"Have you ever been to his room at the Hotel Wagram?"

"Once. I found him with some tart. He threw me out. Then three days later he came around here just as if nothing had happened."

"Does he fish?"

She laughed.

"No! Not with a line."

"Does he play golf?"

"Golf, yes."

"Where?"

"I don't know. I never went with him."

"Would he go away for several days?"

"He'd leave in the morning and come back the same night."

It didn't fit. What he had to find out was a place where Larner was in the habit of staying overnight.

"Besides the two men who slept here, didn't he introduce you to any of his friends?"

"Hardly ever."

"What sort of friends?"

"Mostly at the races—jockeys, trainers."

Torrence and Maigret exchanged glances. They felt they were getting warm.

"Did he do much betting on the horses?"

"Yes."

"Big bets?"

"Yes."

"Did he win?"

"Almost always. He got tips."

"From the jockeys and the trainers?"

"That's what I understood."

"Did he ever mention Maisons-Laffite?"

"He once telephoned me from there."

"At night?"

"After the races."

"To ask you to join him there?"

"I should say not. To break a date with me!"

"He was going to sleep there?"

"I suppose so."

"At an inn?"

"He didn't say."

"Thank you, Adrienne. I apologize for having disturbed you."

She seemed surprised that he wasn't going to take her along with him, could hardly believe that he hadn't been trying to trap her.

"Which one did the killing?" she asked when Maigret was already at the door.

"Charlie. Does that surprise you?"

"No. But I like the other one even less. He's as cold as a crocodile."

She ignored Torrence's salutation, smiled vaguely at Maigret, who bowed almost ceremoniously.

As they were on their way downstairs, the Superintendent said:

"We'll have to have her phone tapped. Not that it will get us anywhere. These fellows are suspicious."

Then, remembering how both Pozzo and Luigi had been at great pains to put him on his guard against killers, he added:

"You'd better keep an eye on her. She's not a bad sort, and it would be a pity if anything happened to her."

Pozzo's restaurant was only a stone's throw away, with Lucas still staked out nearby. Maigret had the car drive down Rue des Acacias.

"Nothing to report?"

"One of the guys you described, who shot craps, went in about fifteen minutes ago."

They were just opposite the restaurant. Maigret allowed himself the pleasure of stepping calmly out of the car and going in, touching two fingers to the brim of his hat.

"Greetings, Pozzo."

Then, turning to the man sitting at the bar:

"Your identification card, please."

The man looked like a night-club musician or a gigolo. He hesitated, seemed to glance inquiringly at Pozzo, but Pozzo was looking the other way.

Maigret jotted down the name and address in his notebook.

Surprisingly, he was neither Italian nor American, but a Spaniard, and, according to his card, a singer by profession. He lived in a small hotel on Avenue des Ternes.

"Thank you."

Maigret returned the card, asked no questions, touched his hat as he had before, while the Spaniard and Pozzo stupidly watched him leave.

─────────Five─────────

Bundled up in his overcoat, warm and snug in the back of the car, Maigret sat ruminating as he watched the lights flash by. When they were crossing Place de la Concorde he spoke to the driver:

"Go around through Rue des Capucines. I want to make a phone call."

It was a call to the Quai des Orfèvres, and it wouldn't have taken five minutes to drive straight there. But, to tell the truth, he wasn't sorry to have an excuse for returning to the Manhattan Bar in a better frame of mind than he had been in that morning and, besides, having got back his taste for whisky, the idea of having another shot was not disagreeable.

The place was crowded, and at least thirty heads were lined up along the bar in a fog of cigarette smoke. Every one, or just about, spoke English, and several customers were absorbed in American newspapers. Luigi and two bartenders were busy mixing drinks.

"The same whisky I had this morning," Maigret said, and the proprietor was struck by his little air of quiet cheerfulness.

"Bourbon?"

"You served me yourself this morning. I don't know."

Luigi didn't seem pleased to see him, and Maigret thought he caught him giving his customers a quick survey, as if to make sure there was nobody there the Superintendent should not see.

73

"Tell me, Luigi . . ."

"Just a second . . ."

He was serving drinks right and left, bustling about more than was necessary, as if anxious to discourage questions by the police.

"I was saying, Luigi, that there's another compatriot of yours I'd like to meet. Have you ever heard of a certain Mascarelli, also known as Sloppy Joe?"

He had spoken in a normal tone of voice, though others around him were shouting to make themselves heard. Yet at least ten people turned around curiously. He felt like the gentleman who in a gathering of old ladies has inadvertently said a dirty word.

As for Luigi, he abruptly rejoined:

"I don't know him and don't want to know him."

Maigret went to the telephone booth.

"Is that you, Janvier? Will you see if the Baron is still in the building? If he is, ask him to wait there for me. If not, try to get him on the phone and tell him to go to the Quai as soon as possible. It's absolutely necessary for me to speak to him."

He threaded his way through the groups who stood drinking, went back to finish his whisky, then noticed a face he had seen before: a tall blond fellow who seemed right out of an American movie, who had been following him with his eyes.

Luigi was too busy to say good-by. Maigret went out, got into his car, and half an hour later, when he walked into his office, someone got up from the one easy chair in the room.

He was a man they called "the Baron," not because he was a baron, but because that was his name. He did not belong to Maigret's squad. For twenty-five years he had specialized in the race tracks and preferred to remain a simple inspector all his life rather than change to any other kind of police work.

"You asked for me, Superintendent?"

"Sit down, old man. Excuse me a minute . . ."

Maigret took off his overcoat, went into the next room to see if there were any messages, finally settled himself behind his desk and filled his pipe.

After years of frequenting the race tracks, where he was assigned to mix, not with the hoi polloi, but with the habitués of the paddock, the Baron had finally come to resemble them. Like them, he wore his field glasses slung on a strap across his shoulder, and on the day of the Grand Prix sported a pearl-gray derby and spats to match. There were those who claimed they had seen him wearing a monocle. It was perfectly possible. It was also possible, as rumor had it, that he had developed a passion for playing the ponies himself.

"Let me explain the situation, and you tell me what you think."

Maigret in the course of his police career had passed through almost all the divisions. He'd worked on the highways, in railway stations and department stores, and, much to his disgust, on the Vice Squad, but he had never had anything to do with the race tracks.

"Suppose an American who's been living in Paris for two years and who frequents the races regularly . . ."

"What kind of American?"

"Not one who gets invited to receptions at the embassy. A big-time swindler—Bill Larner."

"I know him," Baron calmly remarked.

"Good. That will simplify matters. This morning, for certain reasons, Larner found it necessary to go into hiding, together with two of his compatriots who landed only recently and who don't speak a word of French. We have their descriptions, and I doubt if they've taken a train or a plane. I even doubt if they've gone very far from Paris. Something seems to be keeping them here. They haven't an automobile of their own but are expert at borrowing the first one they come across and then abandoning it later."

Baron was listening attentively, with the air of a specialist called in for consultation.

"I've run into Larner a few times, always with good-looking girls."

"I know. He was hiding out with one of them until today, he and his two pals. I hardly think he'd try the same trick twice."

"I don't either. He's smart."

"I was told by this same woman that he had friends among the jockeys and the trainers. You see what I'm getting at? He must have had to make a quick decision, finding a hiding place at a moment's notice. It is more than likely that he turned to one of his compatriots. Do you know many Americans in the racing world?"

"There are some. Fewer than English, though. But wait. I remember a jockey, young Lope. No, come to think of it, he must be racing in Miami now. I also met a trainer, Teddy Brown, who's in charge of the stable of one of his compatriots. There must be others."

"Hold on, Baron. It would have to be someone who lives in an absolutely safe place. In my opinion, you should put yourself in Bill Larner's shoes, ask yourself where you'd be sure of being out of danger. I've heard he's spent the night at Maisons-Laffitte on occasion, or near there."

"Not so stupid."

"What's not stupid?"

"There are a good many stables around there. Do you have to have the answer right away?"

"As soon as possible."

"In that case, I'll have to hang around certain bars I know to refresh my memory. These fellows come and go. If I have an answer tonight, where can I reach you?"

"At my home."

He started toward the door, looking very important, and Maigret, after a slight hesitation, stopped him.

"Another thing. Watch your step. When you get a tip, don't go to the place yourself. We're dealing with killers."

He couldn't help pronouncing the word with a certain irony, for hadn't he been having it drummed into him for the last thirty-some hours?

"I understand. I'll almost certainly phone tonight. At least I'll have something by tomorrow morning. Will it be all right if it costs a few rounds?"

When Maigret arrived at his apartment on Boulevard Richard-Lenoir, he found Madame Maigret dressed to go out. He had been looking forward to going right to bed, with a hot grog and an aspirin, hoping to cut the cold that was beginning to annoy him, but he remembered now that it was Friday, and that Friday was their night for the movies.

"How's Lognon?" his wife asked.

He had received the latest news. It had turned out that Old Grouch really had pneumonia, which they hoped to check with penicillin, but the doctors were more worried about the blow to his head.

"There's no fracture, but they're afraid of a concussion. By four o'clock he was slightly delirious."

"What does his wife say?"

"She claims they haven't the right to separate people who have been married for thirty years, insists on having him brought home or else on being allowed to stay at the hospital."

"Will they let her do that?"

"No."

Maigret and his wife were in the habit of strolling peacefully, arm in arm, to Boulevard Bonne-Nouvelle, and it didn't take them long to decide on a film. Maigret was not difficult in the matter of films. In fact, he preferred ordinary films to super productions and, slouched in his seat, he would watch the images flow by without paying the least attention to the story. The more unpretentious the theater, the thicker its atmosphere, with an audience laughing at the right moments, eating ice cream and peanuts, and lovers taking advantage of the darkness, the happier he was.

The damp cold persisted. When they came out of the theater, they went to a café for a glass of beer, sitting on the terrace near a brazier, and it was eleven by the time they opened the door of the apartment, and heard the telephone ringing.

"Hello! Baron?"

"This is Vacher, Superintendent. I came on duty at eight o'clock. I've been trying to reach you since nine."

"Something new?"

"An express letter for you. A woman's handwriting. It has 'very urgent' written in enormous letters. Shall I open it and read it to you?"

"Please."

"One second. Here it is:

Dear Superintendent,

I simply must see you right away. It's a question of life or death. Unfortunately, I can't leave my room and I don't even know how I'll get this message to you. Can you come to the Hotel de Bretagne, Rue Richer, almost directly opposite the Folies-Bergère? My room is number 47. Don't tell anybody. There's probably someone watching the hotel.

Please, please come.

The signature, which was hardly legible, began with an *M.*

"Mado, probably," Vacher said. "I'm not sure."

"What time was the letter mailed?"

"At ten past eight."

"I'm going. Nothing else? No news from Lucas or Torrence?"

"Lucas is at Pozzo's. Seems Pozzo made him come in, said it was stupid hanging around on the street when it was warmer inside. He's waiting for instructions."

"Tell him to go to bed."

Madame Maigret, who had been listening, sighed without protesting when Maigret picked up his hat. She was used to it.

"Do you think you'll be back tonight? Anyway, you'd better take a scarf."

He gulped down some brandy before leaving, had to walk to Place de la République before finding a taxi.

"Rue Richer, opposite the Folies-Bergère."

He knew the Hotel de Bretagne, where the first two floors were reserved for what hotel owners call "casuals," prostitutes who bring in a customer for an hour or a moment. The other rooms were rented by the week or by the month.

The theater was closed and the street deserted except for a few persistent women hopefully walking up and down.

He shrugged, entered a badly lighted hall, and tapped on the glass panel of a door to the right. A light went on.

"Who is it?" mumbled a sleepy voice.

"For number 47."

"Go on up . . ."

Through the curtain he could vaguely make out a man lying on the camp bed near the key rack. The man started to stretch out his hand toward the switch that opened the second door. But his hand stopped in midair. It had taken him a while to collect his wits, and at first number 47 meant nothing to him.

"There's no one there," he growled, lying down again.

"One moment. I have to talk to you."

"What do you want?"

"Police."

Maigret thought it better to turn a deaf ear to the mutterings coming from the cubicle, for they were anything but friendly. The man got off the cot, where he'd been sleeping in his clothes. Glowering, he came and unlocked the door. Finally, he looked at Maigret and scowled even more.

"You're not from the Vice Squad, are you?"

"How do you know there's no one in 47?"

"Because the man hasn't been there for days, and the woman left a little while ago."

"When?"

"I don't know exactly. Maybe half past nine."

"Is her name Mado?"

The man shrugged his shoulders.

"I'm only on at night and I don't know the names. She left her key as she went out. Look! There it is on the rack."

"Was the lady alone?"

He didn't answer at once.

"I'm asking you if she was alone."

"What do you want of her? Oh, all right! No use getting mad. Someone went up to her room a few minutes before."

"A man?"

The night man seemed amazed that in a house like this anyone should be naïve enough to ask such a question.

"How long did he stay upstairs?"

"About ten minutes."

"Did he ask you for the number?"

"He didn't ask anything. He went up without even looking at me. At that hour the doors aren't locked."

"How do you know he went to number 47?"

"Because he came down with her."

"Do you have the registration slips?"

"The proprietress has them locked up in her desk."

"Where is the proprietress?"

"In bed with the proprietor."

"Give me the key to number 47 and go and wake her. Tell her to meet me up there."

The man gave Maigret a queer look and sighed.

"You're a brave man. Are you sure you're from the police?"

Maigret showed him his badge and, taking the key, started upstairs. Number 47 was on the fifth floor, a commonplace room with an iron bed, a washbasin, a bidet, a dilapidated armchair, and a chest of drawers.

The bed was still made. There was a newspaper spread out on the dubious counterpane, with pictures of Charlie Cinaglia and Tony Cicero on the first page. It was the final edition, which had come out about six o'clock. The caption included the request that anyone who might have seen the two men or had any knowledge of them should get in touch with Superintendent Maigret at once.

Was that why the woman, who was apparently called Mado, had sent him an express letter?

There were two suitcases in a corner of the room. One was old and well worn and one was brand-new. Both had labels of a Canadian transatlantic company pasted on them. They were not locked. Maigret opened them, began laying the contents on the bed, lingerie, various feminine garments, most of them practically new, all of them purchased in Montreal shops.

"Make yourself right at home!" said a voice from the doorway.

It was the proprietress, slightly out of breath from climbing the stairs. She was small and hard, and her gray hair was done up on metal curlers, which did nothing to improve her appearance.

"And first of all, who are you, anyway?"

"Superintendent Maigret, Crime Squad."

"What do you want?"

"I want to know who the woman is who has been living in this room?"

"Why, what's she done?"

"I advise you to give me her registration slip without arguing."

She had brought it with her, just in case, but she now held it out to him grudgingly.

"You'll never learn manners, the lot of you."

She walked over to a half-open door with the evident intention of closing it.

"One moment. Who occupies that room?"

"The woman's husband."

"Leave the door alone. I see that the couple is registered under the name of Perkins, Monsieur and Madame Perkins of Montreal, Canada."

"So?"

"Did you look at their passport?"

"I wouldn't have taken them if their papers hadn't been in order."

"According to this, they arrived one month ago."

"Have you any objection?"

"Will you please describe John Perkins."

"A little dark man, sickly looking, with bad eyes."

"What makes you say he had bad eyes?"

"Because he always wore dark glasses, even at night. Has he done something wrong?"

"How was he dressed?"

"Everything new from top to toe. That's natural enough for newlyweds, isn't it?"

"They were newlyweds?"

"I think so."

"What makes you think so?"

"They practically never left their rooms."

"Why two rooms?"

"That's none of my business."

"Where did they have their meals?"

"I didn't ask them. Monsieur Perkins must have eaten here, because I almost never saw him go out in the daytime, especially lately."

"What do you call lately?"

"The past week. Or the last two weeks."

"Didn't he ever go out for a breath of fresh air?"

"Only at night."

"With dark glasses?"

"I'm just telling you what I saw. You don't have to believe me if you don't want to."

"She used to go out to buy food. I even came up to make sure they weren't cooking, because that isn't allowed in this hotel."

"So that for weeks he ate nothing but cold meals."

"Seems so."

"Didn't you think that strange?"

"With foreigners you see stranger things than that."

"Your night man told me that Perkins had left the hotel several days ago. Can you remember just when you saw him last?"

"I don't know. Sunday or Monday."

"He didn't take any luggage with him?"

"No."

"Did he tell you he was leaving?"

"He didn't tell me a thing. He could have told me anything at all and I wouldn't have been the wiser, since he didn't speak a word of French."

"And his wife?"

"She speaks French like you and me."

"Without an accent?"

"She has an accent like a Belgian accent. The Canadian accent, they say."

"They had a Canadian passport?"

"Yes."

"How did you know that Perkins had left?"

"He went out for a walk one evening—Sunday or Monday, as I told you—and the next day Lucile, who does the rooms on this floor, said he wasn't there, and his wife seemed worried. If you're going on asking me questions, I might as well sit down."

She seated herself with dignity, looking at him disapprovingly.

"Did Perkins have any callers?"

"Not to my knowledge."

"Where is the telephone?"

"In my office, and I'm there all day. They never telephoned, either of them."

"Did they get any letters?"

"Not a single letter."

"Did Madame Perkins go to the poste restante for mail?"

"I didn't follow her. Say, are you sure you have the right to search their things like that?"

For Maigret, while talking, had gone on emptying the two suitcases, and their contents were now spread out on the bed.

The clothes were neither expensive nor cheap, but of fairly good quality. The shoes had extremely high heels, and the lingerie would have been more suitable for a dance hostess at a night club than for a bride.

"I'd like to see the other room."

"Isn't it a bit late in the day to ask my permission?"

She followed him, as though to prevent him from making off with anything. Here, too, there were brand-new suitcases, bought in Montreal, and all the clothes bore the labels of Canadian firms. It was as if the couple had suddenly decided to start all over again from scratch, and in a few hours had bought everything they needed for the voyage. On the chest of drawers there were a dozen or more American newspapers, ones that were to be found only on Place de l'Opéra or Place de la Madeleine.

Not a single photograph. Not a piece of paper. At the very bottom of one of the suitcases Maigret found a passport in the name of Mr. and Mrs. John Perkins, of Montreal, Canada. According to the dates on the visas, the couple had sailed six weeks before from Halifax and had landed at Southampton, then entered France via Dieppe.

"Did you find what you wanted?"

"Does the chambermaid, Lucile, live in the hotel?"

"She sleeps on the seventh floor."

"Will you ask her to come down."

"Why not? It's so handy being a policeman. You can get people out of bed at any hour of the night, keep them from their sleep and . . ."

She was still grumbling to herself as she started upstairs.

Maigret picked up a bottle of blue ink that had evidently been used to write the letter. He also found some cold cuts left on the window sill to keep cool.

Lucile was a dark little thing and cross-eyed, with a habit of letting one flabby breast pop out of her sky blue bathrobe.

"I won't need you any longer," Maigret said to the proprietress. "You can go back to bed."

"You are really too kind! Don't let him upset you, Lucile."

"No, madame."

Lucile was not in the least upset. The door had hardly closed when she exclaimed ecstatically:

"Are you really the famous Superintendent Maigret?"

"Sit down, Lucile. I want you to tell me all you know about the Perkinses."

"Well, I always thought they were a funny sort of couple."

She managed to blush.

"Don't you think it funny, too, when married people sleep in separate rooms?"

"Didn't they ever sleep in the same bed?"

"Never."

"Are you sure they didn't get together at night?"

"Well, you see, we chambermaids know right off by the way the beds are in the morning, if . . ."

She blushed more than ever, pushing her breast back inside her bathrobe.

"In other words, your impression is that they were not sleeping together?"

"I am almost sure of it."

"What time did you make up their rooms?"

"That would depend on the day. Sometimes about nine o'clock in the morning, sometimes in the afternoon. I tried to do her room when she was out. But he was always in his."

"What did he do with himself all the time?"

"He'd read those enormous newspapers of I don't know how many pages, did crossword puzzles, too, and wrote letters."

"You saw him writing letters, did you?"

"Yes. Quite often."

"He never went out during the day?"

"Only at first. Not for the last two weeks, I'm sure."

"Wasn't there something wrong with his eyes?"

"Not when he was in his room. He never wore his glasses when he was in here, but he'd put them on to go to the toilet at the other end of the hall."

"In other words, he was hiding?"

"I think so."

"Did he seem frightened?"

"That's what I thought. Whenever I'd knock, I could hear him jump, and I'd have to say my name before he'd unbolt the door."

"And was she like that too?"

"It wasn't the same thing, not until Monday, that is."

The breast was out again, pale and limp.

"Or, rather, since Tuesday morning. It was Tuesday when I noticed that Monsieur Perkins wasn't here."

"Did she tell you he'd gone away on a trip?"

"She didn't tell me anything. She wasn't the same. Several times she asked me to go and buy her food at the delicatessen. This evening . . ."

"It was you who mailed the express letter?"

"Yes. She rang for me. I used to run all her little errands, and she always gave me good tips. I'd buy the newspapers for her, too."

"Did you bring her this evening's paper?"

"Yes."

"Did she look as if she were planning to go out?"

"No. She was undressed."

"And when she gave you the letter?"

"She was wearing a housecoat. See, there it is hanging on the hook."

"What time did you go up to bed?"

"At nine o'clock. I begin work at seven in the morning. I shine all the shoes on three floors."

"Thank you, Lucile. If you happen to think of anything else, telephone me at the Quai des Orfèvres. In case I'm not there, leave the message with the inspector who answers the phone."

"Yes, Monsieur Maigret."

"You can go back to bed now."

She hung around a few moments longer, smiled at him, murmured:

"Good night, Monsieur Maigret."

"Good night, Lucile."

He went down a few minutes later and found the night man waiting for him, with a bottle of red wine in front of him.

"Well, what did the boss have to say?"

"She was very nice," replied the Superintendent. "So was Lucile."

"Did Lucile try to make up to you?"

A habit of the chambermaid, no doubt?

"Do you always come on duty at nine o'clock?"

"Yes. But I don't go to bed until eleven, even later, not until the Folies closes up."

"Did you get a good look at the man who came for Madame Perkins?"

"Only through the curtain, but good enough."

"Will you describe him?"

"A tall blond guy with a fedora pushed back on his

head. He didn't have any overcoat, and that's what struck me, because it's cold.''

"Perhaps he had a car out front."

"No. I could hear them walking away on the sidewalk."

This detail about the overcoat seemed to remind Maigret of something, but what it was he couldn't recall for the moment.

"Did she seem to go with him quite willingly?"

"What do you mean?"

"Did she open the office door?"

"Well, she had to open it to give me her key."

"Did the man stay outside?"

"Yes."

"He didn't seem to be threatening her?"

"He just stood there peaceably smoking his cigarette."

"She didn't leave any message?"

"No. She just handed me her key and said, 'Good night, Jean.' That was all."

"Did you happen to notice how she was dressed?"

"She was wearing a coat that was kind of dark and a grayish hat."

"She didn't have any luggage?"

"No."

"When her husband went out at night, did he sometimes take a taxi?"

"I always saw him leave and come back on foot."

"Did he go far?"

"I don't think so. He was never gone for much more than an hour."

"Did they ever go out together?"

"When they first came."

"Not for the last two weeks?"

"I don't think so, no."

"Did he always wear his dark glasses?"

"Yes."

Upstairs, number 47 and the adjoining room both overlooked the street. If the woman never went out with the so-called Perkins, it must have been because she kept watch to see if the coast was clear. Perhaps they had some sort of signal to let him know when he got back whether it was safe for him to come in or not.

The description of Perkins, except for the clothes, was very like that of Mascarelli, nicknamed Sloppy Joe.

Didn't his disappearance Monday night indicate that he might very well be the unknown man who had been thrown out of an automobile onto the sidewalk of Rue Fléchier, almost at poor Lognon's feet?

Maigret took a photograph of Bill Larner out of his pocket, and showed it to the night man.

"Do you recognize him?"

"I've never seen him before."

"You're sure this wasn't the man who came for Madam Perkins?"

"Positive."

Maigret showed him the two other photographs, of Charlie and of Cicero.

"How about these?"

"Don't know them. I read about them tonight in the paper."

Maigret had not kept his taxi. He began walking toward Faubourg Montmartre in the hope of finding one there. He hadn't gone a hundred yards before he became aware that he was being followed.

He stopped, and automatically the sound of footsteps some distance behind him also stopped. He started walking again, and the sound echoed. Abruptly, he turned on his heel, and someone more than fifty yards behind him did the same.

He could make out only a vague form in the shadow of the buildings. He could not very well start running. He could not call out to his unknown shadow, either.

When he got to Faubourg Montmartre, instead of hailing a taxi, he went into an all-night bar, where two or three prostitutes were waiting, without much hope.

Convinced that the unknown man was outside, watching for him, he ordered a small glass of wine and went to the telephone booth.

Six

The police station of the third district was only a few doors from the glaringly lighted bar Maigret had entered, and if it hadn't been for the overzealous Lognon, this district would have taken charge of the case, since Rue Fléchier, where the body had been dumped, was just within the limits of its territory.

Looking worried, Maigret dialed the number.

"Hello! Who am I speaking to? This is Maigret."

"Inspector Bonfils, Superintendent."

"How many men are at the station with you, Bonfils?"

"Only two, Big Nicolas and Danvers."

"Now listen carefully. I am at the Bar du Soleil. A man's been following me."

"What's he look like?"

"I have no idea. He's been careful to keep in the shadow and far enough away so I couldn't even make out his build."

"Do you want us to grab him?"

Irritated, Maigret nearly replied like Pozzo, like Luigi: "We're not dealing with amateurs!"

"Listen carefully," he said. "If this fellow came up to the window and saw me go to the telephone booth, he knows what's up and may have run off by now. Even if he didn't see me, he'd probably guess that I'd telephone and . . . What's that?"

"I said that people don't always think of everything."

These people do. Anyway, he's on his guard."

Though he couldn't see Bonfils's expression, Maigret was sure it was slightly ironic. What a fuss over questioning a fellow on the street when he wasn't expecting it. It was simple routine. It happened a dozen times a day.

"You're staying in the bar, Chief?"

"No. There are still people going by. I'd rather this operation take place on a deserted street. Rue Grange-Batelière would be the place. It isn't long and it won't be difficult to close off both ends. Send two or three men in uniform to Rue Drouot immediately. Warn them not to show themselves and to keep their revolvers ready."

"As serious as that?"

"Probably. Nicolas and Danvers are to station themselves on the steps of Passage Jouffroy. I suppose by this time the gates of the passage are closed?"

"Yes."

"Better repeat their instructions twice, rather than once. In ten minutes I'll leave here and walk slowly toward Grange-Batelière. I'll go a little beyond the entrance to the passage, but the men aren't to budge. When my shadow reaches them, they're to jump him. Be careful! He is certainly armed."

Maigret added, knowing very well that it would make the Inspector smile:

"If I'm not mistaken, he's a killer. As for you, Bonfils, take several uniformed men and cut off Rue de Faubourg Montmartre."

It isn't often that such forces are mustered to arrest one man, and yet at the last moment, Maigret added:

"Just to be on the safe side, have a car parked on Rue Drouot."

"Speaking of cars, Chief . . ."

"What is it?"

"There's probably no connection, but I'd better tell you, just in case. Has this man been following you long?"

"From Rue Richer."

"Do you know if he came there by car?"

"No, I don't."

"About half an hour ago, one of our men spotted a stolen car on Faubourg Montmartre, a little above Rue Richer. Its description was broadcast early in the afternoon."

"Where was it stolen?"

"At the Porte Maillot."

"Did your man pick it up?"

"No. It's still in the same place."

"It's not to be moved. Now, repeat the instructions."

Like a good pupil, Bonfils repeated them, including the word "killer," which he pronounced after just a suspicion of a pause.

"Will ten minutes be enough for you?"

"You might make it fifteen."

"I'll leave here in fifteen minutes. Remember, everybody armed!"

He himself was not armed. He went over to the bar and, because of his cold, drank a hot grog, turning his back on the women watching him hopefully.

Now and then a couple went by outside. It was one o'clock in the morning, and most of the taxis were headed for the Montmartre night spots. His eye on the clock, Maigret drank another grog, buttoned up his overcoat, opened the door, and, with his hands in his pockets, strolled down the street. Since he was retracing his steps, his shadow should have been in front of him, but he saw no one. Had the man passed the bar while he was in the telephone booth?

Maigret was careful not to look back, played all his trump cards, walking with unhurried steps, even stopping under a streetlight as though to consult his notebook.

The stolen car was still parked at the curb, and there was no policeman in sight. In all, there were not more than a dozen people on the street, which was filled for a moment with the boisterous shouts of a happily inebriated group.

Until he reached Rue Grange-Batelière, Maigret would not know whether he was being followed, and when he at last turned into it, he felt a sudden tightening of his throat. He had gone about fifty yards when he thought he heard footsteps rounding the corner behind him.

Now everything depended on Big Nicolas, a regular giant, whose greatest joy in life was a good free-for-all. Maigret did not turn his head as he walked past Passage Jouffroy, but he knew that there were two dark figures crouched on the steps that separated the sidewalk from the closed passage. Two or three windows of the hotel opposite were still lighted.

He walked on, smoking his pipe, and calculated that the man must be almost up to the passage entrance. Another dozen steps . . . Now he had reached it. . . .

Maigret listened for the sound of a struggle, of bodies rolling on the street. What stopped him in his tracks was the sudden report of a gun, without the anticipated sounds.

He wheeled around, saw, in the middle of the street, a short, stocky man shooting a second time, then a third, in the direction of the passage.

A whistle shrilled at the corner of Faubourg Montmartre: undoubtedly, Bonfils warning his men.

Rue Grange-Batelière was guarded at both ends. A body had rolled down the steps, probably Big Nicolas, because, stretched out on the sidewalk, it looked enormous. And the other man, Danvers, had begun shooting too. The men at the corner of Rue Drouot came running up now. One of them started shooting much too soon, and a bullet came within an inch of hitting Maigret. Then a police car drove up.

The killer had practically no chance of escaping, and yet, by the strangest fluke, the miracle occurred.

Just when the policemen were closing in from both sides, a vegetable truck came around the corner of Rue Drouot going, God knows why, in the direction of Faubourg Montmartre on its way to the Halles. It was tearing along, making a terrific noise. The driver had no idea what was going on. He must have heard the shots. One of the policemen shouted something at him, probably ordering him to stop, but, suddenly seized with panic, he stepped on the gas instead and went charging down the street.

The unknown man, taking advantage of this lucky chance, leaped onto the back of the truck. Danvers kept firing at him, and Nicolas, prone on the sidewalk, was shooting too.

Nevertheless, it still looked like victory for the police, because the police car was following. But before it had reached the corner of Faubourg Montmartre, one of its tires was hit by a bullet and collapsed.

Bonfils, who had darted back out of the way of the truck, was blowing his whistle more frantically than ever, hoping to alert any policemen who might be on duty on the Grands Boulevards. But they knew nothing of what was happening. They saw the truck race by and wondered what they were expected to do. The terrified pedestrians had started running when they heard the shots.

Maigret knew now that the game was up. Leaving Bonfils to continue the chase, he approached Big Nicolas and bent over him.

"Wounded?"

"Right in the belly!" the man growled, his face contorted.

A van from the police station arrived, and a stretcher was taken out.

"You know, Chief, I'm sure I got him, too," Nicolas said as they hoisted him into the van.

It was true. When, with a flashlight, they examined the street where the gangster had stood during the encounter, they found traces of blood.

From a distance came two or three more shots, on the other side of the Grands Boulevards, toward the Halles. There, the man had every chance of making his escape. At that hour, trucks were coming in from the country in

every direction, and fruits and vegetables were being un-
loaded in the middle of the street. The whole neighborhood was clogged. Hundreds of poor devils hung around
waiting for a chance to lend a hand and earn a little money,
and drunks straggled out of the cheap bars.

Dejectedly, Maigret walked toward the police station
and went into Bonfils's office. There was a little stove in
the middle of the room and, automatically, he began putting on more coal.

The station was almost empty. There were only a sergeant and three men left. They didn't dare ask questions,
and their attitude was one of stupefaction.

Things were not happening in the usual way. The chips
had come down too soon, with disconcerting precision
and ruthlessness.

"You've alerted the Emergency Squad?" Maigret asked
the sergeant.

"Just as soon as I got the word. They've thrown a cor-
don around the whole neighborhood."

That was routine. It wouldn't do any good. If the fellow
had succeeded in escaping almost a dozen armed men in
a deserted street guarded at both ends, he would certainly
have no trouble disappearing in the teeming confusion of
the Halles.

"Aren't you going to wait to hear what happens?"

"Where did they take Nicolas?"

"To Hôtel-Dieu Hospital."

"I'm going to the Quai des Orfèvres. Keep me posted."

He took a taxi and, going through the market district,
was stopped twice by cordons of police. They had begun
the roundup. Prostitutes were scampering away in every
direction to escape it. A Black Maria was parked near one
of the pavilions.

Pozzo and Luigi had not been so far wrong. Maigret
had known it from the beginning. Cinaglia and Company
were not novices, or amateurs. They seemed to foresee
every move of the police and acted accordingly.

Slowly, he climbed the main stairway and went through the inspectors' office, where Vacher, who still hadn't heard of the new developments, was busy making coffee on a hot plate.

"Will you have some, Chief?"

"With pleasure."

"Did you find the Mado woman?"

But, after a glance at the Superintendent, he decided he'd better not ask any more questions.

Maigret had taken off his overcoat. Without knowing it, he had kept his hat on and had sat down at his desk, where he began absently playing with a pencil.

Barely conscious of what he was doing, he dialed his own number, heard his wife's voice saying:

"Is that you?"

"I won't be home all night, probably."

"What's the matter?"

"Nothing."

"You seem out of sorts. Is it your cold?"

"Perhaps."

"Anything wrong?"

"Good night."

Vacher brought him a cup of steaming coffee, and he went to his closet, where he always kept a bottle of Cognac.

"Would you like some?"

"A drop in my coffee wouldn't do any harm."

"The Baron hasn't phoned?"

"Not yet."

"Do you have his home number?"

"I jotted it down."

"Call him."

This worried him too. The Baron had promised to telephone, and it wasn't likely that he was still on the prowl at this hour.

"No one answers, Chief."

"And Lucas?"

"I sent him home to bed as you told me to."

"Torrence?"

"He followed the woman to the Folies-Bergère, afterward to a brasserie on Rue Royale, where she had supper with a woman friend. Then she went home alone, and Janvier is still watching the house."

Maigret shrugged. What was the good of all this, since his opponent was always one jump ahead? He gritted his teeth as he thought of Pozzo and his advice, of Luigi's patronizing attitude. They both seemed to say:

"You're a good fellow, Superintendent, and here, in Paris, against second-rate criminals you're tops. But this is no job for you. These guys play a rough game, and they may hurt you. Drop it! What business is it of yours, anyway?"

He called the Hôtel-Dieu, had some difficulty getting anyone who could give him the information he wanted.

"They are operating now."

"Serious?"

"Laparotomy."

Lognon, taken for a ride, beaten up in the Forest of Saint-Germain, and almost finished by a blow to the head from the butt of a gun! Big Nicolas, with a bullet in his belly before he'd had time to budge!

In other words, even while he was following Maigret on Rue Grange-Batelière, the man expected an ambush and had his gun in his hand ready to shoot. It was a miracle that Danvers hadn't got hit too.

Judging by his build, it must have been Charlie. And Charlie, who hardly knew Paris, who didn't speak a word of French, nevertheless came and, single-handed, pulled one off in the very heart of the city.

Mascarelli, the man they called Sloppy Joe, had left Montreal under an assumed name, in the company of a woman with whom he was not apparently on intimate terms.

The other two, Charlie and Cicero, had sailed openly

from New York under their own names, like people who had nothing to fear, and it was also under their own names that they had registered at a hotel on Rue de l'Etoile.

Did they know in advance what they were coming for? Probably. They also knew whom they could count on to help them.

Maigret would have sworn that it was not without reluctance that a man like Bill Larner, who had never employed strong-arm methods, had agreed to work with them.

Some way or other, they had secured his collaboration, had sent him to a garage to rent an automobile.

Did they already know Mascarelli's address when they landed? It wasn't at all sure, since they had waited two weeks before attacking him.

They did nothing lightly, waited coldly until they had all the trumps in their hand.

During the two weeks they had been preparing to strike, they had probably gone to Pozzo's restaurant with Larner.

Had they also frequented the Manhattan? It was possible. But Luigi, honest as he was, would not have told Maigret. Hadn't he spoken with a certain insistence of American businessmen who preferred paying the racketeers to being shot?

As for Sloppy Joe, he seemed to have been tipped off. During the last two weeks, that is, ever since the arrival of the other two men, he had redoubled his precautions.

It was a poker game in which you staked your life and in which each player seemed to guess the cards held by his opponent.

Sloppy Joe in his hotel on Rue Richer knew he was threatened and he holed up, going out for a short time only at night, decked out in dark glasses like a film star.

Charlie and Cicero must have been watching his movements for several days, preparing their trap, and that Monday night, in the car Larner had rented, were lying in wait for him near the Hotel de Bretagne.

It must have happened exactly as it had with Lognon,

the car driving up to the curb, the revolver leveled at Mascarelli . . .

"Get in!"

In the heart of the city, at a time when there was still considerable traffic on the streets. Had they taken him to the country before shooting him? Probably not. It was more likely they had used a silencer. A few moments later they were dumping his body onto the sidewalk of Rue Fléchier.

Maigret kept doodling on a piece of paper like a schoolboy in the margin of his exercise book.

Just as the car was starting off, Charlie or Cicero must have caught sight of Lognon's shadowy form. It had been too late to shoot. And besides, at that moment, it no longer mattered whether the body was discovered or not, since the job was done.

On all these points, Maigret was sure he was not mistaken. The car drove around the neighborhood, came back a few minutes later, and the two men saw that the body had been taken away. It could not have been the police. They would have been slower about it; there would have been more red tape. But there wasn't a soul on the sidewalk.

Who had whisked away the body?

"They are professionals," Luigi had stated emphatically.

They had acted like professionals. Suspecting that the man they had caught a glimpse of had taken down their license number, the next day they had kept watch on the garage that had rented them the car, then followed Lognon, probably expecting to find the wounded man, or the body, at his place.

Charlie and Cicero, who didn't speak a word of French, were unable to question either the concierge or Madame Lognon.

So they sent Larner.

They must have been dismayed to learn that the man on

Rue Fléchier was actually a police inspector, and wondered why nothing appeared in the papers.

It was, of course, of capital importance for them to find their victim, dead or alive. At the same time, now that they knew that the police were on their track, they had to get out of circulation.

It was as if from then on they had foreseen all Maigret's slightest moves and parried them.

They had left their respective hotels, then, after Pozzo's warning, had abandoned their refuge on Rue Brunel.

Photographs of the men appeared in the papers. A few hours later, Sloppy Joe's companion disappeared from the Hotel de Bretagne. And when Maigret left the hotel, he was trailed by Charlie Cinaglia, who, on Rue Grange-Batelière, did not hesitate to start a fight in the well-known Chicago manner.

"Vacher!"

"Yes, Chief . . ."

"Will you make sure the Baron isn't home yet."

This business of Baron's silence had him more and more worried. The Inspector had told him that he was going to hang around certain bars frequented by the racetrack crowd.

Maigret did not underestimate his adversary. Baron might perhaps learn something. But wouldn't the others, by the same token, realize that he was on their trail? Wouldn't the same thing happen to Baron that had happened to Lognon?

"There's still no answer."

"Are you sure you have the right number?"

"I'll check."

Vacher called information, and was told the number was correct.

"What time is it?"

"Five to two."

It had just occurred to Maigret that the Manhattan was one of the bars frequented by people interested in racing.

It might still be open. If not, it was possible that Luigi was still there checking his cash.

Sure enough, Luigi himself answered the phone.

"This is Maigret."

"Ah!"

"Are there still people there?"

"I closed ten minutes ago. I'm alone. I was just leaving."

"Tell me, Luigi, do you know an inspector they call 'the Baron'?"

"The racetrack cop?"

"Yes. I'd like to know if you saw him tonight?"

"I saw him."

"What time?"

"Let me see. The bar was still crowded. It must have been about eleven-thirty. Yes. Just after the theaters closed."

"Did he talk to you?"

"Not to me personally."

"Do you know whom he talked to?"

There was a silence at the other end of the wire.

"Listen, Luigi. You're a decent fellow, and there's never been a thing against you."

"Well?"

"One of my men just got a bullet in his belly."

"Is he dead?"

"They are operating right this minute. A woman has disappeared from her hotel room."

"You know who she is?"

"Sloppy Joe's companion."

Silence again.

"The Baron didn't go to your place just for a drink."

"I'm listening."

"It was Charlie who shot my inspector."

"Have you arrested him?"

"He got away, but with some lead in him too."

"What do you want to know?"

"I haven't heard from the Baron and I must find him."

"How do you expect me to know where he went?"

"Perhaps if you told me whom he talked to this evening, it would put me on the right track."

Another silence, longer this time.

"Listen, Superintendent, I think you'd better come here for a moment, so we can have a little chat. I'm not sure whether it's really worth your while, because I don't know much. . . . On second thought, we'd better not meet here. You never can tell."

"Will you come to my office?"

"No, thanks. I think not! Let's see. If you'll go to La Coupole, Boulevard Montparnasse, and make sure nobody's tailing you, I'll meet you in the bar."

"How long will you be?"

"Long enough to close up and get there. I have my car outside."

Before leaving, Maigret called the hospital again.

"There's a chance he'll pull through!" he was told.

After that he had Bonfils on the wire.

"You didn't get him?"

"No. Half an hour ago, we got a report about a car stolen on Rue de la Victoire. I've broadcast the number."

Always the same tactic.

"Say, Bonfils, did you examine the other car, the one left on Faubourg Montmartre?"

"I thought of that. It's been in the country today. There's some fresh mud on it. I telephoned the owner, and he says it was clean this morning."

Maigret got into one of the police cars outside, after waking its sleeping driver.

"La Coupole."

Luigi was there ahead of him, having a couple of sausages with a glass of beer at a little table near the bar. There was scarcely anyone in the place.

"You weren't followed?"

"No."

"Sit down. What will you have?"

"The same."

It was the first time Maigret had seen Luigi out of his own place. He looked serious, worried. He began talking in an undertone, without taking his eyes off the door.

"I don't like getting mixed up in affairs like this, I don't like it at all. On the other hand, I'd have you in my hair if I didn't."

"Unquestionably," Maigret replied coldly.

"This morning, I tried to put you on your guard. Now it seems it's too late."

"Yes, the chips are down, and the game will be played to a finish. What do you know?"

"Nothing definite. All the same, it might possibly give you a lead. Any other night, I probably wouldn't have paid any attention to the Baron. But his being in my place to-night struck me because he was the second . . ."

He looked as if he'd like to bite off his tongue.

". . . the second cop today," Maigret finished for him.

He added:

"Had the Baron been drinking?"

"Well, he wasn't exactly sober."

It was one of the Inspector's weaknesses, but he didn't often lose his self-control.

"He sat alone for quite a while just watching people. Then he went over and spoke to a certain Loris, who used to be a trainer for one of the Rothschilds. I don't know what they talked about. Loris likes to drink. In fact, that's why he lost his job. They were at the very end of the bar against the wall. Later I saw them go over to one of the tables at the back, where Loris introduced the Baron to Bob."

"Who is Bob?"

"A jockey."

"American?"

"He lived in Los Angeles for a long time, but I don't think he's an American."

"Does he live in Paris?"

"Maisons-Laffitte."

"That's all?"

"Bob made one, maybe several, telephone calls, out-of-town calls, probably, because he asked me for quite a number of tokens."

"Enough to call Maisons-Laffitte, for instance?"

"Could be."

"Did they all leave together?"

"No. I didn't notice them for quite a while. As I said, it was the rush hour after the theater. When I looked over at their table again, Bob and your friend were alone."

Maigret didn't know just how all this added up, and Luigi motioned to the waiter for two more beers.

"There was a customer at the bar who kept watching them," Luigi went on.

"Who?"

"A young man who's been coming in for an occasional whisky the last few days. As a matter of fact, he was at the bar this morning when you were there."

"A tall blond man?"

"He told me to call him Harry. All I know is that he's from St. Louis."

"Like Charlie and Cicero," growled Maigret.

"Exactly."

"He didn't ask you about them?"

"He didn't ask any questions. The first day he stopped for a moment in front of that picture of Charlie in boxing trunks and sort of smiled."

"Could he hear what Bob and the Baron were saying?"

"No. He seemed satisfied just to watch them."

"Did he follow them when they left?"

"We haven't got that far. Remember I'm only telling you what I saw. I'm drawing no conclusions. It's already too damn much, and I'd rather know that Charlie was dead than wounded. Bob came to ask me if I'd seen Billy Fast."

"Who's Billy Fast?"

"A kind of bookmaker who lives somewhere in Maisons-Laffitte. He was downstairs. I don't know if you've ever been down there. It's a little room under the bar where regular customers get together."

"I know."

"Bob went down alone. Then he came to get your inspector, and I didn't see them again for quite a while. Finally, a good quarter of an hour later, I saw the Baron crossing the large room toward the door."

"Alone?"

"Alone. He was pretty loaded."

"Very drunk?"

"Drunk enough."

"And your customer at the bar, the tall blond man from St. Louis?"

"That's just it. He left right after him."

Maigret thought that was all, and looked dejectedly at his glass. What he'd just heard had some meaning, but it was extremely hard to fathom.

"That's really all you know?"

Luigi looked at him hard for a moment before replying:

"Do you realize I may be risking my hide?"

Maigret thought it wiser to say nothing and wait.

"It's clearly understood that I haven't told you a thing, that I haven't seen you tonight, that, no matter what happens, you won't call me as a witness?"

"It's a promise."

"Billy Fast does not live right in Maisons-Laffitte, but, mostly, at an inn in the forest near there. I've heard it mentioned occasionally. As far as I can make out, it's a place where certain people go when they want some country air. It's called Au Bon Vivant."

"Is it run by an American?"

"An American woman who used to be a chorus girl and is soft on Billy."

As Maigret started to take his wallet out of his pocket,

Luigi waved it aside with what was more a grimace than a smile:

"Nothing doing! This is on me! People might say I let the police buy me drinks. How much, waiter?"

They were equally worried.

Seven

When Vacher saw Maigret walk into the office, he knew right away that something was up, but he also knew that it was no time to ask questions.

"Bonfils phoned a few minutes ago," he said. "The man got away. One of the market women says she noticed him behind a pile of baskets and that he threatened her with his revolver to keep her quiet. It's probably true, because they found traces of blood on one of the baskets. On Rue Rambuteau, he bumped into a tart, who says he was holding one shoulder higher than the other. Bonfils thinks that instead of trying to get out of the neighborhood right away, he stayed there for quite a while, watching every move of the police and changing his place accordingly. They're still patrolling the district."

As though not listening, Maigret had taken an automatic out of the drawer and was examining it to make sure it was loaded.

"Do you know if Torrence is armed?"

"Probably not, unless you gave him a specific order."

Torrence always insisted that his two fists were better than any weapon.

"Get me Lucas on the wire."

"But you only sent him home a couple of hours ago."

"I know."

The Superintendent's look was heavy and his voice dragged, as if very weary.

"Is that you, Lucas? Sorry to wake you, old man. I

thought you wouldn't be pleased if, by any chance, we reached the finish tonight and you weren't in on it.''

"I'm on my way, Chief.''

"Not here. You'll make better time if you jump into a taxi and meet me at the corner of Grande-Armée and Brunel. I have to go there to pick up Torrence. By the way, better bring your revolver.''

After a slight hesitation, Lucas said:

"But Janvier?''

And, that, only a few at the Police Judiciaire would have understood. Even before his chief mentioned a revolver, Lucas had known that it was serious. Maigret was phoning him, was going to pick up Torrence, too, taking him off surveillance, and automatically Lucas thought of Janvier, the other loyal friend, as though it would be unheard of that any expedition take place without him.

"Janvier is home. It would take too long to go for him.''

He lived in the suburbs in the opposite direction from where they were going.

"Can't I come along?'' asked Vacher timidly.

"And leave nobody on duty?''

"Buchet's in his office.''

"I can't leave the entire responsibility on him. And you, do you know Maisons-Laffitte?''

"I've often driven through, and I've been to the races a few times.''

"Do you know the country around there, toward the forest?''

"I used to go there with the kids sometimes.''

"Have you ever heard of a place called Au Bon Vivant?''

"There are a good many places everywhere with that name. The simplest thing would be to phone the district police. Do you want me to get them?''

"On no account! Nor the local police. Nor anybody at all. And don't breathe the name Maisons-Laffitte in front of anyone! Is that clear?''

"Yes, Chief."

"Good night, Vacher."

"Good night, Chief."

Maigret had hesitated, glancing toward the closet where the bottle of Cognac was kept. His pockets were already weighted down with two automatics. Outside, he asked the policeman who was driving:

"Armed?"

"Yes, Superintendent."

"Have you any children?"

"I'm only twenty-three."

"That means nothing."

"I'm not married."

He was a policeman of the new school, who looked more like an Olympic champion than like one of the old constables one used to see on street corners, with their paunches and their big moustaches.

A fairly stiff, very cold wind had risen, and it gave an odd character to this night. There were two distinct banks of clouds in the sky. The lower one, thick and dark, driven swiftly before the wind, made the darkness for the most part complete. But occasionally there would occur a sudden rent, and then you could see, as though through a crack between two rocks, a lunar landscape where, very high, fleecy, moonlit clouds stood motionless.

"Don't drive too fast."

He wanted to give Lucas, who lived on the Left Bank, time to get to Avenue de la Grande-Armée. At first, Maigret had thought of accepting Vacher's offer. He had even thought of taking along Bonfils, who would have liked nothing better.

But he realized the responsibility he was assuming, and the nice mess he might be getting himself into.

First of all, he had no right to be operating around Maisons-Laffitte, which was outside his jurisdiction. According to regulations, he should have referred the case to Rue des Saussaies, which would have sent men of the Sûreté, or he'd have had to obtain letters rogatory for the police of Seine-et-Oise, which would have taken hours.

If only from the point of view of prudence, considering what he knew of his opponents and what had just happened on Rue Grange-Batelière, a massive operation would seem to be indicated. But that, Maigret was convinced, would be one sure way of inviting bloodshed.

That's why he had chosen Torrence and Lucas. He would have added Janvier if it had been possible, and also perhaps young Lapointe, for the experience.

"Turn down Brunel and stop when you see Torrence."

He was there, pacing up and down.

"Get in. Are you armed?"

"No, Chief. The dame isn't dangerous, you know."

Maigret handed him one of the two guns he had, while the car drew up to the curb at the corner of the avenue.

"You got a tip? Are we going to arrest them?"

"Probably."

"If she'd had her way, you wouldn't have found me here."

"Why?"

"Because I'd be in the lady's bed. Even before we left for the theater, she started working on me.

" 'Why don't you ride in the same taxi with me,' she says. I didn't see any objection, and she sat plastered against me the whole way. 'Aren't you coming in to see the show?' I thought I'd better keep an eye on her dressing room. I only watched from the wings while she was on. We came back together."

"She didn't talk?"

"Only about Bill Larner. I think she's on the level about not knowing the others, and she swears she's scared of them. She took a girl friend with her to get a bite to eat on Rue Royale. She invited me, too, but I declined. Then we came back here alone and we stood in the doorway quite a while, like a pair of lovers.

" 'Don't you think you could watch me better up in my room?' she said.

"But I was on to her. What would you have done in my place? I'm not saying I would've minded . . ."

Maigret suspected Torrence of deliberately rattling on because of the air of tension. A taxi stopped directly behind the police car, a door banged, and Lucas came eagerly toward them.

"We're going after them?"

"You didn't forget your gun?"

And, to the driver:

"Maisons-Laffitte."

They went through Neuilly, then Courbevoie. It was three-thirty in the morning, and they kept passing trucks going to the Halles, big lumbering trucks, fast express trucks, very few private cars.

"Do you know where they're hiding out, Chief?"

"Maybe. It isn't certain. The Baron promised to call me but he didn't. I'm afraid he may have had the same idea as Lognon, and decided to carry on alone."

"Was he drinking?"

"Apparently."

"Did he have his car?"

Maigret frowned.

"He has a car?"

"For a week or more. A convertible he bought second hand. He runs around in it all over."

Didn't that explain the Inspector's silence? When he'd left Luigi's bar, excited by all the drinks he'd had and seeing his car at the door, hadn't he suddenly decided to run out to Maisons-Laffitte to find out for himself if the tip was good?

Then Lucas asked:

"Did you telephone the local police?"

Maigret shook his head.

"Does Rue des Saussaies know about this?"

"No."

They understood each other, and for some time there was an impressive silence.

"Are there still three of them?"

"Unless they've separated, which I don't believe. Charlie's wounded. As far as we know, he got a bullet in one shoulder."

Maigret briefly described the fracas on Rue Grange-Batelière, and they listened like men sizing up a situation.

"He seems to have come back to Paris alone. You think he came for the woman?"

"It looks that way. He seems to have been too late."

"If he expected to do the job by himself, he couldn't have thought it very difficult."

To tell the truth, they were all worried, because they felt that they were on unfamiliar ground. Ordinarily, they could tell in advance and almost to a certainty what an adversary's reactions would be. They were familiar with just about every kind of criminal.

But these Americans employed methods that baffled them. They acted more quickly. And it was this very quickness of decision that seemed to be their chief characteristic. At the same time, they never hesitated to show themselves, as if the fact that the police knew their identity, as well as their activities, was a matter of complete indifference to them.

"Do we shoot?" asked Torrence.

"If absolutely necessary. I'm not anxious to have a corpse on my hands."

"Have you some idea of how we're going to manage it?"

"Not the slightest."

He knew only that he was fed up and that he wanted to finish it one way or another. These people from the other side of the Atlantic had brought down a man right in the heart of Paris, they had beaten up Lognon, they had picked off a policeman point-blank, without counting the woman they had kidnapped opposite the Folies-Bergère.

In spite of the photographs in all the papers, in spite of the descriptions that had been sent to police all over the country, those men were calmly going about their business as if they were at home, in a city they hardly knew, stealing any automobile that happened to be at hand whenever they needed one, as naturally as they would hail a taxi.

"What shall I do now?" the driver asked as they were driving over the bridge and could see the lights of Maisons-Laffitte.

They caught sight of the chateau and the pale splotch of the race track in the moonlight. The streets were deserted, with only a few lighted windows here and there. They had to locate the Bon Vivant, and the simplest thing would be to ask at the police station they were just passing.

"Go on. There's a grade crossing a little farther along."

By luck, there was a light in the gatekeeper's cottage. Maigret got out of the car, went in, and found a man with an enormous mustache in intimate conversation with a bottle of wine.

"Do you know an inn called Au Bon Vivant?"

There followed endless explanations. Maigret lost track of all the cross streets, the turns to the right and the turns to the left, and had to call in the driver.

"You go through the next grade crossing and continue in the direction of Etoile des Tetrons. You got that? Be sure not to take the road to Château de la Muette, but the one just before it . . ."

The driver seemed to understand. Nevertheless, ten minutes later they were lost in the Forest of Saint-Germain, and had to get out at every crossing to try to make out the names on the signposts.

The lower clouds had again closed in, and they had to use a flashlight.

"There's a car parked up the road ahead of us with its lights off."

"We better investigate."

It was standing in the middle of the road, in the middle

of the forest. They started toward it, all four of them, and Maigret cautioned them to keep their guns in their hands. It was one of the smaller roads, and dead leaves crackled under their feet.

It may have been ridiculous to take such precautions, but the Superintendent didn't want to risk his men's lives, so they were more than ten minutes approaching the abandoned automobile.

It was empty. On the plate inside was the name of a businessman with an address on Rue de Rivoli. The flashlight beam, falling on the driver's seat, revealed spots of blood that were still fresh.

Another stolen car!

"You know why they left it here, don't you? The house isn't in sight. If we're where I think we are, and if the gatekeeper was right, the Bon Vivant is at least half a kilometer farther on."

"Will you check the gas, Lucas?"

That was the ridiculously simple explanation. Charlie had taken the first car he came across and had suddenly found himself out of gas. The inside of the car still smelled of cigarette smoke.

"Let's go! The important thing is not to let them hear us coming."

"Do you think the Baron came along here?"

In many places, the road was muddy, but there were too many fallen leaves for them to make out any trace of footsteps or tire marks. And now, besides, they no longer dared to use their flashlights.

They finally came to a turn in the road, with a clearing on the left, and in this clearing they saw light filtering through drawn curtains in two windows. Maigret whispered his instructions:

"You stay here," he said to the driver, "and don't come any nearer unless there's a fight. Torrence, you go around to the back of the house, in case anyone tries to make a break that way."

"Do I shoot at the legs?"

"Preferably. Lucas, you come with me. Stay near the house, but far enough away so you can watch the windows."

It was an impressive moment for the three of them. And yet they had all engaged in more difficult arrests than this. Maigret was thinking in particular of a Pole who had for months terrorized farms in the North and who had finally holed up in a little hotel in Paris. He was armed to the teeth. He, too, was a killer. A man who, feeling himself cornered, might have shot into a crowd, causing a veritable massacre in a final act of bravado.

What in the world was so extraordinary about these men, anyway? It was as though Pozzo and Luigi had finally succeeded in giving Maigret God knows what complex.

"Good luck, boys!"

"Shit!" growled Torrence, touching wood.

And Lucas, who prided himself on not being superstitious, furtively did the same.

As far as they could judge, the Bon Vivant was a former gamekeeper's lodge, comprising not more than three rooms on the ground floor, and the same number upstairs, with a pitched slate roof, barely discernible in a faint ray of moonlight.

Maigret and Lucas crept noiselessly toward the lights on the ground floor, and when they were not more than twenty yards from the house, the Superintendent touched the Inspector on the arm and motioned to him to turn left.

He himself waited a few moments, without moving, until he was sure that each man was in position. Fortunately, the wind, stronger here than in Paris, shook the branches and made the dead leaves rattle along the ground. But for at least two minutes they were all in danger, when, through a rift in the clouds, the moon suddenly illuminated the whole place so brightly that Maigret could see the buttons on Torrence's overcoat, and Lucas's gun, although Lucas was farther from Maigret than Maigret was from the house.

As soon as the clouds closed over the moon again, he took advantage of the darkness to cover the distance between himself and the lighted windows. The nearest one was covered with red-and-white-checked curtains like the ones at Pozzo's, but they were carelessly drawn, leaving a slit through which he could see into the room.

It was the barroom of the inn, with a zinc counter and half a dozen tables of polished wood. The whitewashed walls were hung with cheap pictures. There were no chairs, only rustic benches, and on one of these sat Charlie Cinaglia, his profile toward the Superintendent.

His chest was bare, rather fat, and covered with very black hair that stood out startlingly against the white skin. A big woman with bleached hair was coming in from the kitchen with a steaming pot. Her lips were moving, but her voice was inaudible outside.

Tony Cicero was there too, in his shirt sleeves. On the table, beside a bottle that evidently contained pure alcohol or some other disinfectant, lay two revolvers.

Glancing at the floor, Maigret noticed a basin full of reddish water in which pieces of cotton were floating.

Charlie was still bleeding, and it seemed to worry him. The bullet had hit the tip of his left shoulder and, without penetrating, had, as far as the Superintendent could judge, nipped off a piece of flesh.

None of the three seemed to be worrying about the possibility of an attack. The woman poured hot water into a saucer, added some of the liquid from the bottle, wet a piece of cotton, and applied it to the wound, while Charlie gritted his teeth.

Tony Cicero, a cigar in his mouth, picked up a flask of whisky from the table and handed it to his friend, who took a long pull from the bottle.

Bill Larner was nowhere in sight. Until now, Cicero had not turned his full face toward Maigret, but, when he did, the Superintendent was surprised to see that he had a black eye.

What followed occurred so quickly that no one really knew what was happening.

As he handed the bottle back to Cicero, Charlie had glanced toward the window. Maigret was evidently not as invisible as he thought, for, without the slightest change of expression to show that he was alerted, Charlie had reached out with his good arm, and his hand had touched one of the revolvers.

At the same moment, Maigret had pressed the trigger of his own gun, and, as in a Hollywood film, Charlie's gun fell to the floor, his hand hanging limp.

With the same rapidity, Cicero, without looking around, had overturned the table, using it as a barricade; the woman took two or three steps and flattened herself against the wall near the window, out of the line of fire.

Maigret ducked just in time as a bullet smashed the windowpane and splintered some of the wood.

He heard footsteps to his left, as Lucas rushed up to him.

"Did you get him?"

"I got one of them. Look out!"

Cicero kept on shooting. Lucas began crawling toward the door on his belly.

"What shall I do?" shouted the driver, who was still off behind them.

"Stay where you are."

Maigret raised his head a little, trying to see inside. A bullet whizzed through his hat.

He kept wondering where Bill Larner was and if he would join the party. It was really dangerous; Maigret realized that he might attack them from any direction, shooting, for instance, from one of the upstairs windows, or he might surprise them from behind.

Lucas kicked open the door.

At the same time, a voice from inside gave a kind of war cry. It was Torrence, yelling:

"Go to it, Chief!"

The woman was yelling, too. Lucas charged. Maigret stood up, saw two men wrestling on the floor on the other side of the overturned table, while the woman was in the act of picking up an andiron from the fireplace.

Lucas got to her in time to prevent her from using it, and it was funny to see the little man hanging on to the wrists of the big American woman, who was a whole head taller than he.

The next instant, Maigret was also in the room. On the floor, Charlie was trying to reach one of the revolvers, a few inches away from his hand, and the Superintendent did something he had never done before in his whole career. For once, he let his fury have free rein, bringing his heel down on the killer's hand.

"You filthy beast!" the woman spat at him, while Lucas still clung to her wrists.

As for Torrence, he was bearing down with all his weight on Cicero, who was trying to gouge out his eyes, and Maigret had to make several attempts before he succeeded in snapping handcuffs around the man's wrists.

When Torrence stood up, he was beaming. Dust from the floor streaked his sweaty face, and Cicero had torn his shirt collar and left a nasty scratch on his cheek.

"Don't you want to put the bracelets on her, too, Chief?"

Exhausted, Lucas was asking for help, and it was Torrence's handcuffs that Maigret snapped around the wrists of the Bon Vivant's proprietress.

"You ought to be ashamed of yourself, attacking a woman!"

The driver appeared in the doorway.

"Need any help?"

And Torrence, lifting Charlie by the shoulders, making him wince with pain:

"What shall I do with him, Chief?"

"Sit him over there in the corner."

"When I heard the shots, I decided to come in the back

way. The door was locked. I broke a window and got into the kitchen.''

Still breathing hard, Maigret slowly and meticulously filled his pipe. When he'd got his breath, he went over to a cabinet full of glasses.

''Who wants some whisky?''

But he was still uneasy, and sent the driver outside to make sure no one was trying to leave the house.

To Lucas he said:

''Will you take a look around and see if there isn't another car?''

He glanced into the kitchen, where the remnants of a cold supper were still on the table, opened a door into a smaller room, which was probably used as a dining room.

He started up the stairs, his automatic, still warm, in his hand, stopped on the landing to listen, and with a kick opened another door.

''Anybody here?''

There was nobody. It was the woman's room and, like Pozzo's restaurant, the walls were covered with photographs. There were at least a hundred, of both men and women, most of them inscribed ''To Helen,'' and many of her as a chorus girl, taken at least twenty years ago.

Before studying them, Maigret made sure there was no one in the other rooms. The beds had not been slept in. In one of the rooms he found suitcases full of silk underwear, toilet articles, and shoes, but not a single document.

These were evidently the suitcases Charlie and Cicero had taken with them on their successive migrations. At the bottom of the heaviest one were two more automatics, a silencer, a pair of brass knuckles, and a blackjack, as well as a respectable supply of ammunition.

Of Sloppy Joe's companion not a trace. On the other hand, returning to the kitchen, he found, lying by the coffeepot, a cigarette case marked ''B.L.,'' which seemed to indicate that Larner had been there.

Lucas returned from his tour of inspection, his boot covered with mud.

"No sign of another car anywhere."

Meantime, Torrence had examined the wounded man's hand, which had been pierced by the bullet. Strangely, the wound was not bleeding, a clot having formed on each surface, but the fingers were visibly swelling, turning blue.

"Is there a telephone in the house?"

It was behind the door.

"Call a doctor in Maisons-Laffitte, any doctor, without mentioning the police. Better say there's been an accident."

Lucas nodded, and Maigret, for the first time, and not without hesitation and some embarrassment, tried out his bad English on these men.

He first turned to Cicero, who was seated on a bench, leaning against the wall.

"Where is Bill Larner?"

As he expected, his only answer was a contemptuous smile.

"Bill was here tonight. Did he give you your black eye?"

The smile disappeared, but the mouth remained tightly clamped.

"Have it your own way. I hear you're tough, but we have them just as tough on this continent."

"I want to telephone my consul," Cicero finally said.

"Is that all? At this time of night? And may I ask what you think you'll tell him?"

"Okay. You'll have to take the responsibility."

"That's right. I will. Did you get the doctor, Lucas?"

"He'll be here in a quarter of an hour."

"What was your impression? Will he telephone the Maisons-Laffitte police?"

"I don't think so. He didn't turn a hair."

"I wouldn't be surprised to learn there were some pretty

wild doings in this place sometimes. Will you call the PJ and find out if they have any news of the Baron.''

That still worried him, and also the disappearance of the woman from the Hotel de Bretagne.

''While you're about it, ask Vacher to send along another car. We can't all crowd into ours.''

Then, turning to face Charlie:

''Nothing to tell me?''

The only answer he received was the crudest insult in the English language, an allusion to the manner in which his mother had conceived him.

''What did he say?'' asked Torrence.

''He made a discreet allusion to my parentage.''

Lucas reported, ''Vacher has no news of the Baron, Chief. He just tried his number again a quarter of an hour ago. Seems Bonfils telephoned to report that an automobile was stolen . . .''

''Rue de Rivoli?''

''Yes.''

''Did you tell him we'd found it?''

A car stopped in front of the door, and a man, quite young, came in carrying a black bag. He hesitated when he saw the state of the room, the revolvers on one of the tables, and finally the handcuffs.

''Come in, doctor. Pay no attention. We're the police and we've just had a little argument with these gentlemen and this lady.''

''Doctor,'' she began, ''I want you to tell the Maisons-Laffitte police—they know me—that these brutes . . .''

Maigret introduced himself and pointed to Charlie, who was ready to pass out in his corner.

''I wish you'd fix him up so we can take him back to Paris with us. He was messed up first in Paris, and again in the course of our little discussion.''

While the doctor was looking after Charlie, Maigret made another tour of inspection, taking particular interest in the pictures in the woman's bedroom. Then he went to get one of the suitcases, emptied it, and filled it with all the pictures on the walls, the papers he found in a drawer, letters, bills, newspaper clippings. He put in the cigarette case, and also, after carefully wrapping them, the glasses and cups that had been used.

When he got back to the barroom, Charlie looked groggy, and the doctor explained:

"I thought I'd better give him a sedative, to keep him quiet."

"Serious?"

"He's lost a great deal of blood. Perhaps at the hospital they'll want to give him a transfusion. He's tough."

Cinaglia just sat staring at them stupidly.

"No one else to patch up?"

"You'll have a drink with us, won't you, doctor?"

Maigret knew what he was about.

Afraid the doctor might report to the police at Maisons-Laffitte, he wanted to keep him from leaving until the car Vacher was sending arrived.

"Sit down, doctor. Have you had occasion to come here before?"

"Now and then, haven't I, Helen?"

He seemed to know her very well.

"But never under similar circumstances. Once it was a jockey who had broken his leg and who stayed in one of the rooms upstairs for a month nursing it. Another time I was called in the middle of the night to treat a gentleman who had had too much to drink and whose heart was giving out. I seem to remember a girl, too, who had been hit on the head with a bottle, accidentally, I was told, one night when everyone was a bit excited."

The car came at last. Charlie, whose legs gave way under him, had to be carried. Cicero walked out contemptuously, his hands on his stomach, and, without a word, got into the car.

"Will you go with them, Torrence?"

It was to give him a little well-earned satisfaction, since he'd done the lion's share of the work.

"Too bad it isn't a little later in the day and that Pozzo's restaurant isn't open yet."

Perhaps if it had been nine o'clock, instead of half past four, Maigret would not have been able to resist the temptation of going through Rue des Acacias and inviting Pozzo to come out and take a look at the occupants of the car.

"Leave Charlie at Beaujon Hospital. It will please Lognon to know he's under the same roof. Bring the other to the Quai."

Then, to the woman, whose name was Helen Donahue, according to her papers:

"Let's go!"

She just stared him in the face without moving.

"I said, 'Let's go!' "

"You're not going to make me budge. I'm in my own house. You haven't a warrant. I also insist upon talking to my consul."

"That's all. We'll talk about that later. So you won't come with us?"

"No."

"Ready, Lucas?"

They took hold of her, one on each side, and lifted her bodily. The doctor, who couldn't help laughing at the sight, held the door open for them. She kept struggling so furiously that Lucas lost his hold, and she fell to the ground. He had to call the driver to the rescue.

Finally, they got her to the car, pushed her in as best they could, and Lucas climbed in beside her.

"To the Quai," the Superintendent ordered.

They hadn't gone a hundred yards when he changed his mind.

"Tired, Lucas?"

"Not specially. Why?"

"I hate to leave the place without anyone."

"I understand. I'll get out."

Maigret changed to the back seat and, lighting his pipe, asked politely:

"I don't suppose the smoke bothers you, does it?"

The only answer he received was the same insult of which a short time ago he had given an extremely vague translation.

Eight

Snugly ensconced in his corner, his coat collar turned up, his eyes stinging from lack of sleep and the cold in his head, Maigret, ignoring his companion, stared straight ahead. But they hadn't been driving more than five minutes before she began talking of her own accord, in little snatches, and as though to herself.

"Some policemen I know think they're smart, but they're going to be taught a lesson. . . ."

A long silence. She was probably waiting for some reaction, but the Superintendent was nothing but an inert mass beside her.

"I'm going to tell the consul that these people behaved like savages. He knows me; everybody knows Helen. I'll say they struck me and that one of the inspectors even made passes at me."

She must have been beautiful once. Even at fifty she still had a certain attraction. Was she already drunk when Maigret burst into the inn? Possibly. It was difficult to say. She had the hoarse voice of women who drink and stay up all night, and with that peculiarly vague look in her eyes.

It was amusing the way she sat in sullen silence for a few moments, then muttered a sentence, usually just one, addressed apparently to no one in particular.

"Besides, I'll say they hit a man when he was down. . . ."

Perhaps she was just venting her pent-up rage, but she

might also have been goading Maigret, trying to make him
lose his temper.

"Some people think themselves superior because they
can put handcuffs on a woman who hasn't done anything."

It was so funny at times that the driver had a hard time
keeping a straight face. As for Maigret, he kept puffing
hard on his pipe, trying not to smile.

"I'll bet they won't even give me a cigarette. . . ."

Maigret didn't budge, forcing her to a direct attack.

"Well, have you got a cigarette or haven't you?"

"Pardon me. I didn't know that you were talking to me.
I don't carry cigarettes. I'm a pipe smoker. As soon as we
arrive, I'll find you one."

This time the silence lasted to La Jatte bridge.

"They think nobody in the world is smart but Frenchmen. Still, if Larner hadn't put them wise . . ."

This time Maigret looked at her in the faint light from
the dashboard. Her face revealed nothing, so for some
time he wondered whether she had spoke intentionally.

After all, with that little sentence she had given him an
important piece of intelligence. He had suspected it. From
the beginning, he had had the impression that Bill Larner
was not working with people like Charlie and Cicero of
his own accord. Besides, his part had been confined to
getting a car, to examining Lognon's papers, and, finally,
to taking them to Rue Brunel to one of his friends', then
probably out to the Bon Vivant.

When they'd whisked Lognon off to the Forest of Saint-
Germain, Larner had served as translator, but had not laid
a hand on him.

Tonight, to recover his liberty, he had taken advantage
of the fact that Charlie was in Paris and that he had only
Cicero to deal with. This he probably had been anxious to
do for a long time, especially since things had grown too
hot for him.

Had he told Cicero of his intention? Had Cicero surprised him as he was leaving and tried to stop him? In any case, Larner had hit him. In the face.

"Do you own an automobile?" Maigret asked the woman.

Now that he was asking questions, Helen was silent, once more assuming a scornful expression.

He didn't remember having seen a garage near the inn. Charlie had gone back to Paris in the car that had taken them out to Maisons-Laffitte. Larner must have left on foot through the forest, making for either the highway or the station. He had at least two hours' start, and there was little chance of catching up with him before he crossed the border.

As they were passing a little bistro already open, near the Porte Maillot, Helen said, still not addressing anyone in particular:

"I'm thirsty."

"I have some Cognac in my office. We'll be there in ten minutes."

The car was speeding through the deserted streets. There were a few early risers about already. When the car stopped on Quai des Orfèvres, in the courtyard of the Palais de Justice, Helen, before stirring from her seat, asked:

"Do I really get that Cognac?"

"I promise."

Maigret heaved a sigh of relief. For a moment, he had been afraid they would have to carry her, as before.

"Wait here," he said to the driver.

And, when he started to help her up the stairs, she snapped:

"Don't touch me. I'll also say that you tried to sleep with me."

Was she perhaps playing a part? Perhaps that was what she always did? Playing a part to be able to endure her life?

"This way . . ."

"The Cognac?"

"Yes . . ."

He opened the door to the inspectors' office. Torrence and his prisoner had not yet arrived, having had to stop at the hospital to leave the wounded man. Vacher was there, at the telephone, and he glanced at the American woman with curiosity.

"You say the receiver is off the hook? Are you sure? Thanks."

"One moment," Maigret interposed, as Vacher started to speak. "Keep an eye on her, will you?"

He went into his office, got the bottle of Cognac and some glasses, held out a drink to Helen, who gulped it down and motioned toward the bottle for more.

"Not too much at a time. In a little while. Have you a cigarette, Vacher?"

He slipped one between her lips and held up a lighted match. In return, blowing the smoke in his face, she assured him:

"I detest you all the same."

"Haven't you anyone here who can watch her? We better not talk too much in front of her."

"Why not put her in the cubbyhole?"

What they called the "cubbyhole" was at the top of the stairs, a narrow cell with nothing but a cot and a mattress and no light. Maigret hesitated, decided to lock her up in one of the empty offices.

"The Cognac," she reminded him through the door.

"Later!"

He returned to Vacher.

"What was that about a telephone off the hook?"

"The Baron's. I've been dialing his number about every half hour. Up to an hour ago, the phone rang, but there was no answer. For an hour now, I've been getting a busy signal. It had me worried, so I finally called the operator. She tells me the receiver's been left off the hook."

"Do you know where he lives?"

"Rue des Batignolles. I have the number on my pad. You think you'll go?"

"I think I'd better. Meanwhile, send out a general alarm about Bill Larner. He left the neighborhood of Maisons-Laffitte about three hours ago. The Belgian border's the place to watch particularly. Torrence will be here with Tony Cicero any minute."

"And the other guy?"

"At Beaujon."

"Did you damage him much?"

"Not too much."

"What do they say?"

"Nothing."

Suddenly they looked at each other, listening, and Maigret started for the office in which Helen was locked. In spite of the handcuffs, she was engaged in wrecking the place, sending inkwell, desk lamp, papers, everything she could reach, to the floor.

When she saw the Superintendent, she merely smiled.

"I'm behaving about like you behaved in my house."

"The cubbyhole?" queried Vacher.

"She's asked for it."

On the Pont-Neuf, his car passed the one bringing in Torrence and Cicero, and the drivers exchanged a sign of recognition. When he reached Rue des Batignolles, Maigret noticed a convertible parked with two wheels on the sidewalk and, looking inside, he saw Baron's name on a little plate surmounted by a Saint Christopher medal.

He rang. The concierge, who was still half asleep, released the outer door catch, and Maigret had to stop to ask her, through the glass panel of the door, where the Inspector lived.

"Did he come in alone?" he inquired.

"What business is it of yours?"

"I'm a colleague of his."

"He can tell you himself what he did."

It was one of those apartment houses where several families lived on each floor, working-class families, for the most part, and even at that early hour there were lights in many of them. The contrast was striking between this modest building and the aristocratic airs the Baron tried to emulate. Now Maigret understood why the Inspector, who was a bachelor, never mentioned his private life.

On one of the doors on the fourth floor was a visiting card with Baron's name, but no mention of his profession. Maigret knocked and, receiving no answer, turned the knob.

The door opened, and the first thing he saw was the Baron's hat lying on the floor. After turning on the light, he noticed a tiny kitchen to the left, then a dining room, with a set of Henri II furniture and embroidered doilies such as one still sees occasionally in a concierge's quarters, and finally a bedroom with the door wide open.

The Baron was lying fully dressed across the bed, one arm dangling to the floor, and if he hadn't been snoring, one might have thought he had met with an accident.

"Hey! Baron! Wake up, old man . . ."

He flopped over like a fish, without waking up, and the Superintendent shook him.

"It's me . . . Maigret . . ."

It took several minutes. Finally, the Inspector grunted, half opened his eyes, groaned because the light hurt them, recognized Maigret, and, in a sort of panic, tried to sit up.

"What day is it?"

He probably meant to ask, "What time is it?"

For his eyes began searching for his alarm clock, which had fallen to the floor and was ticking away under the bed.

"Would you like a glass of water?"

Maigret went to the kitchen and when he returned with the water, he found the Inspector looking both miserable and worried.

"Please excuse me . . . Thank you . . . I'm sick. . . . If you knew how awful I feel . . ."

"Perhaps I'd better make you some strong coffee?"

"I'm ashamed. . . . I swear that . . ."

"Lie still."

The apartment was more like that of an old maid than a bachelor, and one could well imagine the Baron coming home from work and donning an apron, to go about his household chores.

This time, Maigret found him sitting on the edge of the bed, looking utterly hopeless.

"Drink . . . You'll feel better. . . ."

Maigret had poured himself a cup of coffee too. Taking off his overcoat, he sat down by the bed. The room reeked of liquor. The Inspector's clothes were wrinkled and filthy, as though he had spent the night under the bridges.

"It's terrible," he sighed.

"What's terrible?"

"I don't know. I have important things to tell you. Terribly important!"

"Well?"

"I'm trying to remember. Tell me what's happened?"

"We've arrested Charlie and Cicero."

"You've arrested them?"

His face betrayed the effort he was making.

"I don't think I've ever been so drunk in my life. I feel really sick. It's something about them. Wait. I remember—they mustn't be arrested."

"Why?"

"Harry told me . . ."

The name came back to him, and that seemed to him a great victory.

"His name is Harry. . . . Wait . . ."

"I'll help you. You were at the Manhattan, Rue des Capucines. You talked to several people and you had a lot of drinks. . . ."

"Not at Luigi's. At Luigi's, I hardly drank anything. It was afterward. . . ."

"Was somebody trying to get you drunk?"

"I don't know. I'm sure it will all come back to me little by little. He told me that they mustn't be arrested because it would be running the risk of . . . Good God! It's so hard to . . ."

"Run the risk of what? It was quite late when you left Luigi's. Your car was at the door. You got in and you must have intended to drive out to Maisons-Laffitte."

"How do you know?"

"Someone, during the evening, probably Lope or Teddy . . . Brown."

"How, damn it, do you know all that? I did talk to them. I remember now. That's what you'd told me to do. I had been to several other bars already."

"Where you drank."

"A drink here and a drink there. That's the way you have to do it. I can't even feel my head any more."

"Wait."

Maigret went to the bathroom, came back with a towel wrung out in cold water, and put it on the Baron's forehead.

"They told you about Helen Donahue and her inn in the forest, Au Bon Vivant."

The inspector looked at him in amazement.

"What time is it?"

"Five-thirty in the morning."

"How did you manage to find out?"

"It doesn't matter. When you left Luigi's and got into your car, somebody followed you, a blond man, very tall and quite young, who must have spoken to you."

"That's true. His name's Harry."

"Harry what?"

"He told me. I'm sure he told me. It's a name of one syllable. The name of some singer."

"He's a singer?"

"No, but he has the same name as a singer. Before I had time to shut the door, he got in beside me. He said:

" 'Don't be scared.' "

"In French?"

"He speaks French with a strong accent, makes lots of mistakes, but you can understand him."

"American?"

"Yes. Wait. After that he said, 'I'm connected with the police in a way. Let's not stay here. Let's drive. Anywhere you like.'

"Then, as soon as I'd started the engine, he explained that he was an assistant district attorney. A district attorney, it seems, is a cross between an examining magistrate and a public prosecutor. In big cities there are several assistant district attorneys."

"I know."

"That's true; you were over there. He asked me to stop so he could show me his passport. When a case is important, the district attorney and his assistants take charge of the investigation themselves. Is that right?"

"Right."

"He knew where I thought of going when I left Luigi's.

" 'You mustn't go to Maisons-Laffitte tonight. It won't do any good. I must talk to you first.' "

"Did he talk?"

"We talked for more than two hours, but that's the hard part to remember. First, we drove around the streets at random, and he gave me a cigar. Maybe it was the cigar that upset my stomach? I felt thirsty. I didn't know where we were, but I saw a place that was open. I think it was somewhere around the Gare du Nord."

"Didn't you suggest that he come to see me at the Quai?"

"Yes, but he didn't want to."

"Why?"

"It's complicated. If only I didn't have such a head! Don't you think a glass of beer would make me feel better?"

"Have you any beer?"

"There must be some on the sill outside the kitchen window."

Maigret drank some too. Ashamed of the disorder of his bedroom, Baron had dragged himself into the dining room.

"I remember certain details very clearly; there are whole sentences I could repeat, but, in between, complete blanks."

"What did you drink?"

"Everything."

"Harry, too?"

"He was always the one who'd look over the bottles behind the bar and choose one."

"Are you sure he drank as much as you did?"

"Even more. He was really stinking. Once, he even fell off his chair, flat on the floor."

"You didn't tell me why he refused to get in touch with me."

"As a matter of fact, he knows you very well and admires you."

"Ah!"

"He even met you at a cocktail party given in your honor in St. Louis and he says he remembers a sort of lecture you gave. He came to France to look for Sloppy Joe."

"Was he the one who picked him up on Rue Fléchier?"

"Yes."

"What has he done with him?"

"He took him to a doctor. Wait! Don't say anything. There's a whole bunch of stuff coming back. Because of the doctor. He told me how he had happened to know the doctor. It was right after the Liberation. Harry, who was in the American army, belonged to I don't know exactly what service stationed in Paris. He wasn't assistant district attorney then. He was having himself a time. One of the people he met was a doctor. I have it! It was because of a girl who didn't want to have a baby and who . . ."

"An abortion?"

"Yes. He didn't use the word. He's awfully prudish. But I knew what he meant. He's a young doctor who hasn't established himself yet. Lives near Boulevard Saint-Michel."

"Is that where Harry is having Sloppy Joe fixed up?"

"Yes. I'm pretty sure he was square with me. He kept saying, 'You must tell Maigret this . . . and this too.' "

"It would have been simpler for him to come and see me."

"He doesn't want to have any official contact with the French police."

"Why?"

"It seemed all very simple last night. I remember telling him he was right. Now it doesn't seem so clear. Ah! Yes. First of all, because you would have to question the wounded man, and then it would get into the newspapers."

"Does Harry know that Cinaglia and Cicero are in Paris?"

"He knows everything. He knows everything like the palm of his hand. He knew about their hideout at the Bon Vivant before I did."

"Does he know Bill Larner?"

"Yes. I think I'm beginning to piece it all together. You see, we were both drunk. He kept repeating the same things over and over again. He seemed to think that, being a Frenchman, I was incapable of understanding."

"I know just what you mean!"

Like Pozzo! Like Luigi!

"They've started a big investigation in St. Louis. As happens periodically, they're trying to clean up the city, get rid of the gangsters. It's mostly Harry's job. Everybody knows who the boss of the rackets is. Harry told me his name, an important fellow, to all appearances a perfectly respectable citizen, and the friend of politicians and police officials."

"The same old story."

"That's what he said. Only, over there, the laws aren't the same as ours, and it's hard to convict anyone. Is that true?"

"It's true."

"No one dares testify against a man like that, because anyone who opens his mouth won't be alive forty-eight hours later."

Baron was happy now. He'd just remembered quite a lot all at once.

"Do you mind if I have some more beer? It makes me feel better. Would you like some too?"

His skin was still a sickly gray, and there were dark circles under his eyes, but the pupils were beginning to show a little spark.

"We went on to some other place because our little bistro was closing. I don't remember where we went. Montmartre, probably. A small night club where there were three or four dancers. One of them, a little brunette, gave Harry the eye and came and sat on his lap almost the whole time. There was nobody in the place but us."

"Did he mention Sloppy Joe?"

"That's what I'm trying to remember. Sloppy Joe's a poor fellow in the last stages of tuberculosis. He's spent his life in the rackets, but he's just a kind of hanger-on. Two months ago a man was killed in St. Louis in front of a night club. If I could only remember the names! Everybody is convinced it was the fellow I just told you about who shot him. There were only two witnesses, one of them the doorman at the night club, and he was found dead in his room the next morning.

"That was when Sloppy Joe decided to beat it, because he was the other witness, and that's always unhealthy."

"To Canada?"

"Montreal, yes. On one side, the district attorney's office was trying to lay hands on him to make him talk; on the other, the gangsters were bent on finding him to keep him from talking.''

"I understand."

"Well, I didn't understand. It seems Sloppy Joe really represents millions. If he talks, a whole criminal organization as well as a powerful political machine will collapse, and I can still hear Harry saying:

" 'Over here, you don't know anything about these things. You don't have anything to compare with these big associations of criminals that are organized like regular business concerns. You have it easy. . . .' ''

Maigret could hear him too. It was a song he was beginning to know by heart.

"In Montreal, Sloppy Joe still didn't feel far enough away from his countrymen. He succeeded in getting a false passport. The passport was in the name of a married couple, so he arranged for a woman to go along with him, thinking this would be an even better way of throwing all the people looking for him off the scent. He persuaded a cigarette girl in a night club to leave with him. She's always dreamed of going to Paris. . . . Excuse me a moment.''

Baron dragged himself to the bathroom, and came back with two aspirin.

"Sloppy Joe didn't have much money. He realized that, even in Paris, they'd get him in the end. So one day he sent a long letter to the district attorney, saying that if they would promise to protect him and would come and get him here and give him a certain amount of money, he would be willing to testify. I may be getting it a little mixed up, but that's the general idea.''

"Did Harry ask you to explain all this to me?''

"Yes. He almost telephoned you. He would have called you this morning if he hadn't found out that I knew the killers' hideout. Because they really are killers. Especially Charlie.''

"How did Charlie and Cicero get on to Sloppy Joe's trail?"

"In Montreal. Through the girl Mascarelli brought over. She has a mother back there, and she was stupid enough to write her from Paris."

"Giving her address?"

"A poste-restante address. But she told her that she lived just opposite a big music hall. When Harry decided to come over to get Sloppy Joe and take him back to St. Louis, he learned that Cinaglia and Cicero had forty-eight hours' start on him."

Maigret couldn't help thinking of the miserable existence poor Mascarelli had led since he left St. Louis, first in Montreal, then in Paris, where he didn't even dare leave the hotel for more than a few moments at night to get a little fresh air.

He understood now why Cicero and Charlie had to have a rented car. For two or three days, they had probably been on watch near the Folies-Bergère, waiting for the right moment to act. By that time, the assistant district attorney was on their heels.

"Harry described the whole thing to me. It was like a movie. He was on foot. He had just turned the corner of Rue Richer when he saw Sloppy Joe get into a car. He knew what that meant. There was no taxi in sight. So he looked in front of the theater for an automobile that wasn't locked."

It was rather amusing to think of the assistant district attorney in a stolen automobile! These Americans, no matter on which side of the law, acted in Paris just as if they were at home. The people on the streets that Monday night never dreamed they were participating in a gangster chase in true Chicago style. And if it hadn't been for poor Lognon, who was standing by the iron fence around Notre-Dame-de-Lorette watching for a small-time cocaine peddler, no one would have known a thing about it.

"Sloppy Joe isn't dead?"

"No. As Harry says, his doctor is 'patching him up.'
A transfusion was absolutely necessary, and it was Harry
who gave I don't know how much blood. He watches over
him like a brother, better than a brother. His whole career,
it seems, is at stake. If he arrives back in St. Louis with
Sloppy Joe alive, if he succeeds in keeping him alive until
the day of the trial, and if his man doesn't lose his nerve
at the last minute and actually appears as a witness, Harry
will be almost as famous as Dewey was after he cleaned
the gangsters out of New York."

"What about the woman? Was it Harry who kidnapped
her?"

"Yes. He was angry with you when he saw Charlie's
and Cicero's pictures in the paper."

It was true, really, that these people, no matter which
side they were on, knew their stuff, both the assistant
district attorney and the killers. They had foreseen how
Mascarelli's companion would react when she saw the
photographs in the paper, had expected her to contact the
police.

And she had done just that by sending the express letter
to Maigret.

Charlie had left the Bon Vivant, alone, to see that she
didn't talk. But a few minutes before he arrived, Harry
had come to take her away and put her in a safe place.

They made themselves perfectly at home! They went
about their business as if Paris were a sort of no man's
land where they could do as they pleased.

"Is she at the doctor's, too?"

"Yes."

"Isn't Harry afraid Charlie might find out the address?"

"It seems he's taken precautions. Whenever he goes to
the place, he makes sure no one's following him and he
has someone there as a bodyguard."

"Who?"

"I don't know."

"Now tell me, exactly what was the message he wanted you to give me?"

"He asks you not to do anything about Charlie and Cicero, at least not for a few days. Sloppy Joe can't be moved for another week. Harry intends to take him to America by plane. Until then, there's still danger."

"If I'm not mistaken, he's letting me know that it's none of my business! Is that it?"

"Just about. He has the greatest admiration for you, is looking forward to seeing you after all this is over, either here or in St. Louis."

"How kind of him! Where did you leave this gentleman?"

"In front of his hotel."

"Do you remember the address?"

"It's somewhere around Rue de Rennes. I think if I went to the neighborhood, I'd recognize the building."

"Do you feel up to going now?"

"If you'll just let me change my clothes."

It was almost daylight. People were beginning to move about in the house, and a radio somewhere was giving the news. Maigret could hear the Inspector splashing about in the bathroom, and when Baron came back to the dining room, he resembled a fashion plate except for his face, which still looked like putty.

He seemed mortified when he saw his car with two wheels on the sidewalk.

"Do you want me to drive?"

"I'd rather take a taxi. But you might get your car parked properly."

They walked to Boulevard des Batignolles, found a taxi.

"Left Bank. Along Rue de Rennes."

"What number?"

"Drive the length of the street."

They wandered around the neighborhood for at least fifteen minutes, while Baron inspected the façades of all the hotels. Suddenly he said:

"That's it!"

"You're sure?"

"I recognize the brass plate on the door."

They went in. A man was wiping up the foyer with a damp cloth.

"Isn't there anyone at the desk?"

"The boss doesn't come down till eight. I'm the night man."

"Do you know the names of the people who live here?"

"They're on the rack."

"Is there an American, a big blond man, quite young, whose first name is Harry?"

"Certainly not."

"Won't you check?"

"I don't have to. I know who you mean."

"How's that?"

"The fellow who came in about four o'clock this morning. He asked for the room number of Monsieur Durand. I told him we didn't have any Monsieur Durand.

" 'And Dupont?' he said.

"I thought he was kidding me, so I tried to ignore him, especially since he seemed pretty drunk."

Maigret and Baron exchanged glances.

"He stood where you're standing now and didn't seem to want to leave. He kept fumbling in his pocket, and finally pulled out a thousand-franc note and handed it to me. He said he was just joking, that a woman was pestering him and he'd popped into the hotel to shake her. He asked me to look outside and see if there was a car anywhere. He hung around for a little while longer; then he left."

Baron was furious.

"He's made a fool of me!" he muttered between his teeth when they were out on the street again. "Do you think he's really an assistant district attorney?"

"It's more than likely."

"Then why did he do that?"

"Because," Maigret answered calmly as he got into a taxi, "these people, the good ones as well as the bad ones, think we're children. In kindergarten!"

"Where do you want to go, Monsieur Maigret?" asked the taxi driver, who had recognized him.

"Quai des Orfèvres."

And, glowering, he slumped down in his corner.

Nine

"The Commissioner's just come in, Superintendent."

"I'm going."

It was nine o'clock, and Maigret's cheeks looked gray in the bleak morning light, and his eyes were a little red. For the last half hour, he had kept his handkerchief in his hand, tired of having to take it out of his pocket every other minute.

Three times he had been informed:

"The woman's making a devil of a row."

"Let her!"

Then an inspector had come to say:

"I opened the door a crack to hand her a cup of coffee and she threw it in my face. The mattress is in shreds, and the stuffing's all over the place."

He had shrugged his shoulders. He had had them telephone Lucas to tell him he need not stay at the Bon Vivant any longer.

"Tell him to go home to bed."

But Lucas, anxious to be in at the finish, had hurried back to the Quai des Orfèvres, his face also covered with a dark stubble.

As for Torrence, he had shut himself up in one of the offices with Tony Cicero and obstinately asked questions, which were answered by a scornful silence.

"You're wasting your time, old man," Maigret had pointed out.

"I know. I enjoy it. He doesn't understand a word I say,

but I can see I have him worried. He's dying for a cigarette and too proud to ask. But he will! He's already opened his mouth once, and closed it again without a word.''

There was a strange excitement in the air, which only those who had worked on the case could understand, the handful of men who were Maigret's intimate colleagues. Young Lapointe, for example, when he arrived at the office, wondered why Maigret and his men were going about their strange task with such grim persistence.

The police stations of the Fifth and Sixth Arrondissements had been alerted.

''A doctor, yes, probably pretty young. He lives somewhere in the neighborhood of Boulevard Saint-Michel, but I don't believe he has a nameplate on the door. The prostitutes must know him. He does abortions occasionally. You'd better question the pharmacists in the district. It is probable that last Tuesday he bought quite a supply of various medicines. And go to the surgical supply firms, too.''

That morning, district inspectors who knew nothing about the case were going from door to door, from pharmacy to pharmacy, without dreaming that their job had anything to do with people who had come all the way from St. Louis to settle old scores.

Another inspector, from the PJ, was at the Ecole de Médecine copying the names of students who had graduated in the last few years. Others were questioning the professors. The Vice Squad was working overtime, waking up prostitutes, who couldn't imagine what was up.

''Ever had an abortion?''

''Say! What do you take me for?''

''All right! Don't get excited! We're not trying to get you into trouble. There's a doctor in the neighborhood who does that sort of thing. Who is he?''

''I only know a midwife. Have you asked Sylvie?''

Counting the border and highway police who were on

the watch for Bill Larner, there were several hundred people mobilized on account of the Americans.

Maigret knocked on a door, closed it after him, held out his hand to the Chief Commissioner of the Police Judiciare, and sank into a chair. For ten minutes, his voice expressionless, he summed up all he knew about the case. And when he had finished, his chief seemed even more embarrassed by it than he was.

"What do you plan to do? Get hold of this Mascarelli?"

Maigret was tempted to. He had had his fill of being treated like a small boy.

"If I do, I'll prevent the assistant district attorney from cornering his gangster boss."

"And if you don't, you can't accuse Charlie and Cicero of attempted murder."

"Obviously. But we still have Lognon. They actually kidnapped Lognon, as they say over there, took him to the Forest of Saint-Germain, and beat him up. They also broke into his house, and, finally, Charlie shot an inspector on Rue Grange-Batelière."

"He will say he was attacked, or that he thought he'd run into an ambush, and appearances are in his favor. His attorney will say that he was walking peacefully along the street when he saw two men about to jump him."

"Well, even if it goes that way, we still have Lognon. And that will cost them several years behind bars, or, at the very least, several months."

The Chief couldn't help smiling at Maigret's stubborn expression.

"The woman is not mixed up in this Lognon business," he again objected.

"I know. We'll have to release her. That's why I'm letting her yell. I haven't a thing on Pozzo, either. But one of these days he'll slip up, and we'll close down his place."

"Angry, Maigret?"

At that, Maigret also smiled.

"Admit, Chief, that they go too far. If it hadn't been for Lognon's misplaced zeal, they would have got away with it right under our noses. Later, the story would have been all over St. Louis. I can just hear them:

" 'But what about the French police?'

" 'The French police? They were completely hood-winked, the French police! . . . Naturally! . . .' "

It was eleven o'clock, and Maigret had just finished trying to pacify Madame Lognon, who was telephoning for the second time that day, when an inspector of the Sixth Arrondissement was put on his wire.

"Hello! Superintendent Maigret? The doctor's name is Louis Duvivier and he lives at 17 *bis* Rue Monsieur-le-Prince."

"Is he there now?"

"Yes."

"Is there anyone with him?"

"The concierge thinks there's been a sick man living in his apartment for several days, and that surprised her because usually he has only women patients. True enough, there's a woman there too."

"Since when?"

"Since yesterday."

"No one else?"

"An American who comes almost every day."

Maigret hung up, and a quarter of an hour later he was slowly climbing the stairs in the doctor's apartment house. It was an old building, without an elevator, and the apartment was on the sixth floor. A bell rope hung down on the left side of the door. He gave it a pull and immediately heard steps inside. When the door opened a crack, he caught a glimpse of a face, shouldered his way in, growling:

"What are *you* doing here?"

He felt like bursting out laughing. The man facing him with an automatic in his hand was no other than a certain

Dédé-de-Marseilles, who liked to play the bully in the dives of Rue de Douai. Dédé just gaped at the Superintendent, not knowing what to say and trying to hide his gun.

"I'm not doing anything, honest."

"Hello, Monsieur Maigret!"

The big blond American, in his shirt sleeves, came out of a room with a sloping ceiling and a skylight like an artist's studio.

His face was a little puffy, his eyes bleary, like the Baron's. But his expression was almost one of elation. He held out his hand.

"I figured I'd talked too much last night and that you'd manage to find my address. Are you angry with me?"

A young woman came out of the kitchen, where she'd been stirring something on the stove.

"Let me introduce you."

"I'd rather you and I went downstairs."

He had caught sight of a bed with someone in it: a dark-haired man who was trying to hide his face.

"I see. Just wait a second."

He came back a moment later with his coat on and his hat in his hand.

"What do you want me to do?" Dédé asked him, but looking at Maigret at the same time.

"Anything you please," Maigret answered. "We have the birds under lock and key."

The Superintendent and his companion were silent on their way downstairs. Outside, they began walking toward Boulevard Saint-Michel.

"Is what you just said true?"

"As far as Cicero is concerned, yes. Charlie's in the hospital."

"Did your man give you my message?"

"How soon can you take a plane with your charge?"

"In three or four days. It depends on the doctor. Are you going to make it difficult for him?"

"Tell me, Monsieur Harry . . . Harry what?"

"Pills."

"Of course. Like the singer! That's what Baron told me. Well, suppose I went to your country and behaved the way you have behaved here?"

"I stand corrected."

"You haven't answered."

"You'd risk getting into trouble, into serious trouble."

"How did you come to know Dédé?"

"After the Liberation, when I used to spend most of my nights in Montmartre joints."

"You hired him to guard your patient?"

"I couldn't stay in the apartment night and day. Neither could the doctor."

"What are you going to do with the woman?"

"She hasn't enough money to go back to Canada. I'm paying her passage. There's a boat sailing day after tomorrow."

They were in front of a bar, and Harry Pills stopped, asked hesitantly:

"Don't you think we might have a drink? I mean, wouldn't you let me . . ."

It was funny to see this tall, athletic young man blushing like a Lognon.

"They may not have whisky," Maigret objected.

"Yes, they have. I know the place."

He gave the order, lifted his glass, holding it in front of him for a moment. Still disgruntled, Maigret looked at him like someone who still has plenty on his mind, and then, half in jest, half in earnest, said:

"To Gay Paree, as you say!"

"Still angry?"

Perhaps to show that he really wasn't as angry as all that, or because he liked Pills, Maigret had another drink. And, because he couldn't leave without paying for his round, he had a third.

"Listen, Maigret, old man . . ."

"No, Harry, I'm doing the talking. . . ."

Toward noon, Pills was saying:

"You see, Jules . . ."

"What's the matter?" asked Madame Maigret. "I'd say . . ."

"That I simply have a cold and that I'm going to bed with a grog and two aspirin."

"You don't want anything to eat?"

He crossed the dining room without replying, went into his bedroom, and began undressing. If it hadn't been for his wife, he might have gone to bed with his socks on.

Well, anyway, he'd shown them . . . Precisely!

8 September 1951